DATE DUE		

ALSO BY HILARY MANTEL

Every Day Is Mother's Day

Vacant Possession

Eight Months on Ghazzah Street

Fludd

A Place of Greater Safety

A Change of Climate

An Experiment in Love

the Giant, O'Brien

the Giant, O'Brien

A NOVEL

HILARY MANTEL

A MARIAN WOOD BOOK
HENRY HOLT AND COMPANY

Henry Holt and Company, Inc.
Publishers since 1866
115 West 18th Street
New York, New York 10011

Library of Congress Cataloging-in-Publication Data
Mantel, Hilary, 1952–
The giant, O'Brien : a novel / Hilary Mantel. — 1st ed.
p. cm.
ISBN 0-8050-4428-0 (hb : alk. paper)
I. Title
PR6063.A438G5 1998 98-10701
823'.914—DC21 CIP

Henry Holt books are available for special promotions and
premiums. For details contact: Director, Special Markets.

First Edition 1998

Designed by Paula R. Szafranski

Printed in the United States of America

All first editions are printed on acid-free paper. ∞

1 3 5 7 9 10 8 6 4 2

For Lesley Glaister

. . . But then,

All crib from skulls and bones who push the pen.

Readers crave bodies. We're the resurrection men.

—GEORGE MACBETH, *The Cleaver Garden*

note

This is not a true story, though it is based on one. The Irish giant Charles Byrne exhibited himself in London in 1782 and died there the following year. He bears little resemblance to the giant of this story, since he probably suffered from a pituitary tumour and may have been mentally retarded.

In this story, when the Giant and his band leave Ireland, they are not fleeing from any particular catastrophe. They are fleeing cyclical deprivation, linguistic oppression, and cultural decline, conditions in which it is hard for a great man like the Giant to flourish.

John Hunter was born near East Kilbride in 1728. He was briefly apprenticed to a cabinet-maker in Glasgow, but in 1748 he went to London and began a dazzling career as surgeon, scientist, and collector, which spanned forty years and made him famous but never rich.

Until the Anatomy Act of 1832, the only way a scientist could obtain corpses for study was by stealing them or getting them from the hangman. The peculiar horror people felt at the prospect of dissection was partly because of its association with crime and disgrace, but also because of religious/folk beliefs about bodily resurrection after the Last Judgement.

The episode of Hunter's inoculation with syphilis is controversial. Some authorities think that he inoculated himself, others that he inoculated an experimental subject. In a spirit of generosity, I've decided to believe both. Hunter's experiment was undertaken in the belief that syphilis and gonorrhoea were different manifestations of one poison. I should add, as a word to the worried, that it took place before he was a married man.

I have taken some latitude in describing Hunter's speculations. For instance, his thoughts about vomiting anticipate the work of François Magendie, another great experimenter.

For information about sundry saints, and for the ballad sung by Claffey, I am indebted to *Irish Eccentrics* by Peter Somerville-Large (Lilliput Press). The Giant's poem about King Herod may be found in Kuno Meyer's *Ancient Irish Poetry* (Constable).

The bones of Charles Byrne may be inspected during the usual exhibition hours at the Museum of the Royal College of Surgeons, Lincoln's Inn Fields, London.

the Giant, O'Brien

one

"Bring in the cows now. Time to shut up for the night."

There came three cows, breathing in the near-dark: swishing with the tips of their tails, their bones showing through hide. They set down their hooves among the men, jostling. Flames from the fire danced in their eyes. Through the open door, the moon sailed against the mountain.

"Or O'Shea will have them away over the hill," Connor said. Connor was their host. "Three cows my grandfather had of his grandfather. Never a night goes by that he doesn't look to get the debt paid."

"An old quarrel," Claffey said. "They're the best."

Pybus spat. "O'Shea, he'd grudge you the earache. If you'd a boil he'd grudge it you. His soul is as narrow as a needle."

"Look now, Connor," the Giant said. His tone was interested. "What'd you do if you had four cows?"

"I can only dream of it," Connor said.

"But for house-room?"

Connor shrugged. "They'd have to come in just the same."

"What if you'd six cows?"

"The men would be further off the fire," Claffey said.

"What if you'd ten cows?"

"The cows would come in and the men would squat outside," said Pybus.

Connor nodded. "That's true."

The Giant laughed. "A fine host you are. The men would squat outside!"

"We'd be safe enough out there," Claffey said. "O'Shea may want interest on the debt, but he'd never steal away a tribe of men."

"Such men as we," said Pybus.

Said Jankin, "What's interest?"

"I could never get ten cows," Connor said. "You are right, Charles O'Brien. The walls would not hold them."

"Well, you see," the Giant said. "There's the limit to your ambition. And all because of some maul-and-bawl in your grandfather's time."

The door closed, there was only the rushlight; the light out, there was only the dying fire, and the wet breathing of the beasts, and the mad glow of the red head of Pybus. "Draw near the embers," the Giant said. In the smoky half-light, his voice was a blur, like a moth's wing. They moved forward on their stools, and Pybus, who was a boy, shifted his buttocks on the floor of bare rock. "What story will it be?"

"You decide, mester," Jankin said. "We can't choose a tale."

Claffey looked sideways at him, when he called the Giant

"mester." The Giant noted the look. Claffey had his bad parts: but men are not quite like potatoes, where the rot spreads straight through, and when Claffey turned back to him his face was transparent, eager for the tale he wished he could disdain.

The Giant hesitated, looked deep into the smoke of the fire. Outside, mist gathered on the mountain. Shapes formed, in the corner of the room, that were not the shapes of cattle, and were unseen by Connor, Jankin, and Claffey; only Pybus, who because of his youth had fewer skins, shifted his feet like a restless horse, and lifted his nose at the whiff of an alien smell. "What's there?" he said. But it was nothing, nothing: only a shunt of Claffey's elbow as he jostled for space, only Connor breathing, only the mild champing of the white cow's jaw.

The Giant waited until the frown melted from the face of Pybus, till he crossed his arms easily upon his knees and pillowed his head upon them. Then he allowed his voice free play. It was light, resonant, not without the accent of education; he spoke to this effect.

"Has it ever been your misfortune to be travelling alone, in one of the great forests of this world; to find yourself, as night comes down, many hours' journey from a Christian hearth? Have you found yourself, as the wind begins to rise, with no man or beast for company but your weary pack-animal, and no comfort in this mortal world but the crucifix beneath your shirt?"

"Which is it?" Jankin's voice shook.

"'Tis the Wild Hunt," Connor said. "He meets the dead on their nightly walk, led by a ghostly king on a ghostly horse."

"I will be feart," Jankin said.

"No doubt," said Claffey.

"I have heard it," Connor said. "But at that, it's one of his best."

They finished debating the tale. The Giant resumed, bringing them presently through the deep, rustling, lion-haunted forest to where they had not expected to be: to the Edible House. From his audience there was a sigh of bliss. They knew edible; they knew house. It had seldom been their fortune to meet the two together.

He mixed his tales like this: bliss and blood. The roof of gingerbread, then the slinking arrival of a wolf with a sweet tooth. The white-skinned, well-fleshed woman who turns to bone beneath a man's caress; the lake where gold pieces bob, that drowns all who fish for them. Merit gains no reward, nor duty done; the lucky prosper, and any of us could be that. Jesu, he thought. There were days, now, when he felt weakness run like water through legs that were as high as another man's body. Sometimes his wrists trembled at the weight of his own hands. A man could be at the end of his invention. He could be told out; and those who have not eaten that day have sharp tempers and form a testy audience. Only last week he had asked, "Did you ever hear the story of St. Kevin and O'Tooles's goose?" and a dozen voices had shouted, "OH, NOT AGAIN!"

A cow, intent on the fire, had almost stepped on his foot. To teach it a lesson, he stepped on its own. "Mind my beast!" Connor cried. The Giant glanced to heaven, but his view was blocked by the roof. Forty years ago Connor's grandad had thatched it, and now it was pickled and black from the fire; when it rained, the rain ran through, and it trickled a dilute sooty brown on the men's heads. Connor had no wife, nor was likely to get one. Nor Pybus, nor Claffey; Jankin, he slightly hoped, would be unable to breed.

Changes were coming; he could see them in the fire and feel them in the whistling draught from every wall. His appetite was great, as befitted him; he could eat a granary, he could drink a barrel. But now that all Ireland is coming down to ruin together, how will giants thrive? He had made a living by going about and being a pleasant visitor, who fetched not just the gift of his giant presence but also stories and songs. He had lived by obliging a farmer who wished a rooted tree lurched up, or a town man who wanted his house pushed down so he could build a better.

Strength had been a little of it, height had been more, and many hearths had welcomed him as a prodigy, a conversationalist, an illustration from nature's book. Nature's book is little read now, and he thought this: I had better make a living in the obvious way. I will make a living from being tall.

He turned to Claffey, who alone of them had a bit of sense. He said, "My mind's made up. It'll have to be Joe Vance."

A day or two after, Joe Vance up the mountain. He had a greasy hat to his head, and a flask of strong liquor bobbing at his thigh on a cord. He was a smart man, convenient and full of quips; he had been agent and impresario to a number of those who had left the district over the last ten years. He knew the art of arranging sea voyages, and had sometimes been on voyages himself. He had been in gaol, but had got out of it. He had married many wives, and some of them were dead; died of this or that, as women do. He had black whiskers, broad shoulders that showed the bones plainly, a bluff, reasonable, manly aspect, and honest blue eyes.

Connor's cabin came into view. It had not the refinement of a chimney—since six months there was not a chimney in miles—but there was a hole made in it; indifferently, the smoke eased itself through both the hole and the thatch, so it appeared the whole house was steaming gently into the rain and mist of the morning.

Joe Vance found the cabin full of smoke, and all of them huddled around a miserable fire. His honest eyes swept over their circumstances. The Giant looked up. He was ridiculous on his stool, his knees coming up to meet his ears. "You should have a throne," Vance said abruptly.

"Of that he is in no doubt," Claffey said.

"Will you be coming on the venture?" Vance asked him.

"He must," Pybus said. "He speaks their lingo. Jabbers in it, anyway. We have heard him."

"Do you not speak English, O'Brien? I thought you were an educated giant."

"I have learned it and forgotten it," the Giant said. "I have sealed it up in a lead box, and I have sunk it in the depth of the sea."

"Fish it out, there's a good lad," Vance said. "If any see it, grapple it to shore. You must understand, I'm not aiming to present you as a savage. Nothing at all of that kind of show."

"Are we going as far as Derry?" Jankin asked. "I've heard of it, y'know."

"Ah, Jankin, my good simple soul," said the Giant. "Vance here, he knows how things are to be done."

"You are aware," Vance said, "that I was agent to the brothers Knife, very prodigious giants who you will remember well."

"I remember them as rather low and paltry," O'Brien said. "The larger of the Knives would scarcely come to my shoulder. As for his little brother—Pocket, I used to call him—when I went to the tavern at ten years of age, I was accustomed to clutch my pot in my fist and ease my elbow by resting it on his pate."

"The Knives were nothing," Jankin said. "Dwarves, they were, practically."

Joe Vance moved his honest eyes sideways. He recalled the Knives—especially Pocket—as boys who could knock down a wall just by looking at it. Pocket was, too, uncommonly keen on his percentages, and once, when he thought he was short-changed, he had lifted Joe's own proper person high in the air and hung him by his belt on a hook where a side of pig was stuck just yesterday. It was with one hand he hoisted him, and that his left; Vance wouldn't easily forget it. Glancing up, he appraised O'Brien, assessing his potential for violent excess. Where he could get away with it, he was this sort of agent; he took twenty shillings in the guinea.

"Now, as to my terms," the Giant said. "Myself and my followers—that's these here about—we must have all comfort and commodity on the journey."

"I am accustomed to booking passage," Joe Vance said, bowing.

"It must be a vessel to surprise the Britons. A golden prow and sails of silk."

"You yourself shall be the surprise," Vance cooed.

"I must have six singing women to go before me."

Vance lost control; it didn't take much. "That's all shite! You, Charlie O'Brien, you haven't tasted meat since last Easter. You live on your hands and knees!"

"True," said the Giant, glancing at the roof. "All six must be queens," he said, smiling; he thought Vance's manners mild enough, and what's to be lost by upping your demands?

"Where would I get six queens?" Vance bellowed.

"That's your problem," the Giant said urbanely. He stretched his legs. The brush of his big toe nearly pitched Jankin into the flame, but Jankin blew on his burnt palms, and licked them, and apologised.

Claffey raised his head. He engaged Vance's eye. He nodded towards O'Brien, and said, "He's dangerous, in a room." He left it at that. On the whole, Claffey did know where to leave things.

The Giant said, "Vance, shall I have coin in my pocket? Shall I have gold in my store?"

Vance held out his hands, palms up. "What Joe Vance can lawfully obtain, you shall share in. The English public, of my certain knowledge, is starved of the sight of a giant. It's a kind of charity, now I think of it, to take a giant over to them." He was smiling with half his face. "Englishmen are a type of ape," he explained. The Giant saw this.

"Not so," he said. "Low in stature, barbarous in manner, incomprehensible in speech: unlettered, incontinent, and a joke when they have drink taken: but not hairy. At least, not all over."

"I have never seen an ape," Jankin said. "Nor dreamt of one. Have I seen an Englishman?"

"They are the ones that ride horses," Claffey said.

"So," Jankin said, "I have seen them."

"What about Connor?" Vance asked. "Are you coming yourself?"

"Connor is a man of wealth and substance," Claffey said. "He has his cows to guard."

Connor's brow creased. He ran his hands back through his hair. "Once, O'Shea came over, sneaking in the night with a basin, and bled my cows to make his Sunday broth. As if he were a Kerryman."

"Yes," the Giant said. "A Kerry cow knows when it's Saturday night." He lifted his head. "Well, this hearth has been our anchor. But now we must be under sail."

When they came down the mountain, their feet sunk in the mud and squally rain blew into their faces. It was the time of year when rats stay in their holes, dogs in their kennels, and lords in their feather beds. Civilly, the Giant carried all their packs, leaving them with their hands free to help them balance if they skidded. A league or so on they came to a settlement, or what had been so recently; what was now some tumbled stone walls, the battered masonry raw, unclothed by creeping green. A few months after the clearance, the cabin walls were already disintegrating into the mud around; their roofs had been fired, and they were open to the sky.

Something small, dog-height, loped away at their approach: hands swinging, back bent.

"A hound or a babby?" Pybus asked, surprised.

The Giant wiped the streaming rain from his face. His quicker eyes discerned the creature as not of this world. It was one of those hybrids that are sometimes seen to scuttle, keen, and scrape in ruins and on battlefields: their human part weeping, their animal nature truffling for dead flesh.

"I'd thought we could take shelter," Claffey said. His fur hat lay on his head like a dead badger, and his best coat had its braid ruined. "Not a roof left in the place."

"I told you not to wear your finery," the Giant said.

"A plague on the whole class of agents," Claffey said. "On agents, bailiffs, and squireens."

"You shouldn't say a plague," the Giant said. "You should say what plague. Say, *May their tongues blister, and the eyes in their head spin in orbits of pus.*"

"You're pernickety in cursing," Claffey said. "I'd curse 'em with a cudgel and split their skulls."

"So would I," said Pybus.

"Cursing," the Giant said, "is an ancient and respectable art. An apt curse is worth a regiment of cudgels." He eased the packs on his shoulders. "Ah well, let's step out for the town."

"The town!" Jankin said. He tried to skip.

When they came to the town, only a youth or two walked out to greet them; there was no clamour of children come to see the Sight. They spotted the youths from a great way off; the road was bare and smooth as a queen's thigh. The Giant gave a great hulloo, greeting them from afar; it whooped over the treeless domain, looping the boys like a rope with a noose.

The Giant slowed, accommodating his stride, as he had to remember to do. The youths met them in a wilderness of splintered wood, the raw wet innards of tree stumps offered up to a blowing, twilit sky.

A whole forest chopped down for profit, and houseless birds shrieking at day's end.

"We have only been walking one day," Pybus said, "and we have come to this."

The Giant looked at him sideways. Already, the journey was bringing out finer feelings in Pybus, which he had not suspected him to possess.

The youths bowed when they drew up to them. "Welcome, mesters. These days, even the beggars give us the go-by."

"Do the blind men visit you?" the Giant asked.

"Yes, they have the kindness. They don't turn back, though they say they can smell disaster. Yet if they have a fiddle, we have no strength to dance."

The youths brought them on to the town. "They are cutting, as you see," one said.

The stench of the wood's fresh blood lay on the damp air, floating about the Giant at chest height.

Jankin gaped. "Where will they go, those persons who live in the woods?" Hastily, he corrected himself. "Those gentlepersons, I ought to say."

"We can't care," one of the youths said harshly. "We have lived beside them and even put out milk for them in better times, but we have no milk now and only ourselves to help us. I've heard they'd bring grain and a piece of bacon or a fowl to those they favour, but that's not our experience. They must shift for themselves, as we must."

"It's stories," Claffey said. "Gentlefolk in the woods, green gentlemen and small—it's only stories anyway."

They looked up at the hillside. It was a face with a smashed mouth, with stumps of teeth. There were no shadows and no shifting lights. It was just what it was, and no more: a devastation. The Giant said, to soften the facts for Jankin, "There are still some forests in Ireland. And to travel doesn't irk the gentry, as it irks us. They are as swift as thought." Then he bit his lip, and grinned, thinking that in Jankin's case that was not very swift at all.

The town was silent, and to the Giant this silence was familiar. It was the hush of famine, the calm that comes when bad temper is spent, the gnawing pain has ebbed, and there is nothing ahead but weakness, swelling, low fever, and the strange growth of hair. Only Jankin sang out: "We are coming to the town, the town."

"Kill that noise," Claffey said. They looked about them. Like a puppy, Jankin crept closer to the Giant's side.

"They have broken you, I see," the Giant said to the youths.

The town was nothing now; two streets of huts, dung heaps steaming outside their doors, their walls cracked and subsiding, their roofs sagging. It was a town with no pride left, no muscular strength to mend matters, no spark in the heart to make you want to mend. The rain had stopped, and the clouds were parting. The rutted road held standing pools, a white hazy sun glowing in their depths.

The children stared as they passed, scratching the bursting pods of their bellies. They gaped at the Giant, but they did not shout. They were weary of wonders. The wonder of a dish of potatoes and buttermilk, that would have made them shout; but for potatoes, it was too early in the year. If O'Brien had been the devil come to fetch them, they would have followed him, bug-eyed, hoping they might dine in hell.

"Where's Mulroney's?" Claffey said. "Where's Mulroney's tavern?"

"Where's anything?" one of the youths said. "Mulroney died while you were away up the mountain. He took a fever. His house fell down." He waved an arm. "There it is."

What—that? That ruin slid into a ditch? Mulroney's, where they used to hold the Court of Poetry, after the big house was destroyed? Mulroney's, where there was no fiddling or singing or vulgar harping, but a correct recitation of the old stories in the old metres? It was a court of crumbling men, their faces cobwebbed, their eyes milky, their hands trembling as they gripped their cups. Bad winters killed them one by one, fluid filling the lungs that had breathed the deeds of kings.

"But that can't be Mulroney's!" Pybus burst out. "What will we do? The Giant must have strong drink! It's a need in him."

"It's sauce to a good story," Jankin said, having often heard this expression.

"Joe Vance will be here presently," the Giant said. "We'll do, till then."

A woman appeared at the door of one of the cabins. She began to step towards them, skirting the puddles, though her legs and feet were bare and muddy already. She approached. The Giant saw her large grey eyes, mild and calm as a lake in August: the fine carving of her lips, the arch of her instep, the freedom of her bones at the joint. Her arms were white peeled twigs, their strong muscles wasted; a young child showed, riding high inside her belly like a bunched fist.

"Good day, my queen."

She didn't greet him. "Can you heal? I have heard of giants that can heal."

"Who wants it?"

"My son."

"What age?"

"Three." Her hair was as fine as feathers, and the colour of ash. "And as for three years I have never eaten my fill, neither has he." Blue veins, thin as a pen's tracing, rippled across her eyelids and marbled her inner arm.

These, the Giant said to himself, are the sons and daughters of gods and kings. They are the inheritors of the silver tree amongst whose branches rest all the melodies of the world. And now without a pot to piss in.

Her hand reached up for his arm. She drew him down the street. "This is my cabin."

Beside it, Connor's was a palace. The roof was in holes and mucky water ran freely through it. The child was in the least wet part, wrapped in a tatter or two. In his fever, he kept tearing the rags from him; with practiced fingers, his mother wrapped them back. His forehead bulged, over sunken, fluttering eyelids. "He is dreaming," the Giant said.

Squatting on her haunches, she gazed into his face. "What is he dreaming?"

"He is dreaming the dreams that are fit for a youth who will become a hero. Others babies dream of milk; his dreams are of fire. He is dreaming of a castle wall and an armoured host of men, himself at the age of eight as strong as any man grown, a gem set on his brow, and a sword of justice in his hand."

She dropped her head, smiling. The corners of her mouth were cracked and bleeding, and her gums were white. "You are an old-fashioned sort, are you not? An antique man. If there were a gem on his brow, I would have sold it. If there were a sword of justice, I would have sold that too. What hope for the future, you'll say, if the sword of justice itself is sold? But it is well known, almost a proverb, that a hungry woman will exchange justice for an ounce of bread. You see, we have no heroes in this town, not anymore. No heroes and no virtues."

"Come away with us," he said. "We are going to England. I am going to the great city of London—it seems that there a man can show himself for being tall, and they'll pay him money."

"Come away?" she repeated. "But you go tomorrow, do you not? Shall I leave my son unburied? I know he will die tonight."

"You have no husband?"

"Gone away."

"No mother or father?"

"Dead."

"No brother or sister?"

"Not one alive."

"Must you measure the ground where they dropped? Will you pace it every day?" He indicated the child. "Will you scour these rags to swaddle the child you are carrying? Come away, lady. There's nothing left for you here. And we need a woman of Ireland, to sit beside me on my throne."

"Who's getting you a throne?"

"Joe Vance. He's shown giants before. He's got experience in it."

"Ah, you poor man," she said. She closed her eyes. "I never thought I should say that, to a giant."

"Don't fear. There is a sea voyage, but Vance has made the passage before."

The child's head jerked, once; his eyes flashed open. He reared up his skull. A thin green liquid ran from the side of his mouth. His mother put her hand under his head, raising it. He coughed feebly, snorted as he swallowed the vomit, then began to expel the green in little spurts like a kitten's sneeze.

"What did he eat?" O'Brien asked.

"God alone knows. Here we live on green plants, just as in my grandfather's time men ate grass and dock. The children have found something that poisons them, and it is always the ones who are too young to explain it—you could ask them to lead you to where they have plucked it, but by the time you know they are poisoned they are too weak to lead you anywhere. Or maybe—I have thought—it's something we give them—some innocent herb—that we can eat, but which murders them."

"That's a hard thought."

"It is. Very hard," she said.

The Giant and his train enjoyed nettle soup, and before the craving became acute Vance appeared with his flasks of the good stuff. Squatting in the cabin of the woman, the Giant told these stories: the earl of Desmond's wedding night, and how St. Declan swallowed a pirate. All the town had come in, some bringing a light and others a turf for the fire, listening to the tales and praying in between them. When the death agony arrived, O'Brien took the child onto his knee, so that the rattle in his throat was interlaced and sometimes overlaid by his light, mellifluous tones, that tenor which surprised the hearers, coming as it did from a man so grossly huge. He tried to fit the cadence of his tale to the child's suffering, but because he was a fallible person there were moments when it was necessary for him to pause for thought; at these times, the mud walls enclosed the horror of labouring silence, the scraping suspension of breath before the rasping cry which brought the babby back to life for another minute, and another. His body sleek with hair, his bones thick as wire, he looked like a mouse under O'Brien's hand.

When the crux came, he cried out once, with that distant, stifled cry that hero babies make when they are still in their mothers' wombs. It was cry of vision and longing, of the future seen plain. When O'Brien heard it he scooped the little body in one hand and placed it in his mother's lap, where within a second the child became a corpse. Within another second a green sludge dripped from the nostrils, leaked out between the thighs, dripped like the sea's leavings even from the cock curled like a shell in its rippling beach of skin.

At once, Pybus began to sing, his high-strung boy's voice rising to the sky. The clouds had no call for it; they sent his song back, stifled, to die between the wasted shoulders and the mud walls. "At least you're not short of water," Claffey said, raising his eyes to tomorrow's certainty of rain.

At dawn, the youths met them and escorted them to the end of the town. "Can't you voyage with us?" the Giant asked. "You're brave boys, and there's nothing here for you."

Joe Vance looked daggers.

"Thank you, sir," the foremost youth said. "We are decided to remain here. A better age may come. Are you a poet, by the way?"

"In a poor sort," the Giant said. "I can make a song. But who can't? As for the old systems, the strict rules, I never learned them, and if I'm honest with you it's a matter of training rather than aptitude. I believe there is no one of my generation who is confident in them. That was the use of Mulroney's, you see, we met the old men there, and we would learn a little."

"Let's get on the way," Joe Vance said. He shifted his feet.

"There was a time when friars walked the roads, disguised as rough working men: friars from Salamanca, from Rome, from Louvain. They have left me with the rudiments of their various tongues, besides a sturdy and serviceable Latin, and a knowledge of the Scriptures in Greek. Travelling gentlemen, all: never more than a night or two under the one roof, but always with time to spare for the education of a giant boy."

Joe Vance reached up, and tugged at his clothing.

"A fly besets me," the Giant said. He pretended to look about. "Or some hornet?"

Joe removed his hand, before he could be swatted. "A honey bee," he said.

That night in his sleep, the Giant sat among the dead, and heard the voices of the old men at Mulroney's: dry whispers, like autumn leaves rubbed in a bag.

two

Scotland, day: the child is alone in the field, the black ruts rising around him: flat on his belly on the damp ground, a vast sky swirling. His chin is on the earth, his body is blue in bits, where he has got his clothes wrong. It is his own task to dress himself, cover himself decently, and if he's cold that's his fault. He has been sent out to scare crows. In other places they have a doll to do it, made of sticks and old clothes. He has heard of it: English luxury. Here old clothes are not wasted.

To scare a crow, jump up, wave arms. Bugger it. Bugger it off.

Up a blade of grass a crawler goes. Little black feet on a sweet, edible stalk. He watches, his brow furrowing; it's apt to cross your eyes. He puts out his finger.

The crawler goes on to it, though it doesn't make a feeling; it is too light, or his finger is too cold? His finger tastes of salt, earth, and shit.

He closes his palm. Then opens it, and teasing with his finger takes off one of the crawler's legs. A time ago, when he first did this, he felt a hot wetness deep inside himself, as if water had begun to run there, above his belly button; but now when he does it he feels nothing at all. He pinches off leg two. He can count; they say he can't, but he can. One leg, two leg, three leg, four. Count, yes; and read, by and by. The crawler goes round and round on his palm. Why didn't it fly away? It had the chance. One leg off, it could have flown. It's kicking now, with what's left. It must have stayed because it liked him, because it was his friend, even despite what he'd done. He didn't mean malice; he only wanted to see what would happen. He would like to give it back one leg, two legs, three. He would like to know, now, if it's alive or dead. He breathes, John Hunter, and the words come out on his breath: "It was a trial. It was nothing cruel."

Crows above. Foreign black hands stretching across the sky. He brushes the crawler away. He stands up. The wind's tooth strikes at him, gnaws and gnaws. He flails his arms. John Hunter, he yells, John Hunter. Bugger off all crows. Over and over he shouts: John Hunter, bugger off crows.

three

My brothers are James, lately dead; John, dead; Andrew, dead. William is living but gone away. My sisters are Elizabeth, dead. Agnes, dead. Isabella, dead. Janet, dead.

I have also one sister living yet. Her name is Dorothea. We call her Dolly, when we are in a lighter mood.

Our family suffers from rotten lungs and rotten bones.

The John who is dead is not to be confused with me, the younger John. I say this because though in most cases the dead and the living are quite unalike, there are special circumstances when it is difficult to distinguish one from the other. There are many accounts, some from antiquity, of unfortunate people buried alive. Such burials may be the origin of quaint stories,

stories of vampyres and ghouls and hauntings; of voices from underground, and the earth welling with fresh blood. But I have been in a small room with many a dead man and woman. I have slept under a dissecting bench in brother Wullie's workroom, and I have hauled many a corpse to its final resting place on Wullie's narrow bench. I can tell you that there are no ghosts. If there were, they'd haunt Wullie, would they not?

And haunt me. But don't think it. It's a slab of butcher's meat you have to haul, head waddling and hands flapping; the rigor's passed by the time their keepers knock at the door, and they've once again a semblance of flexible life, yet they're heavy, they don't help you, you have to drag them, and their faces are fallen in, their noses are rims, sharp edges of falling flesh, and their lips are invisible already, shrunk back against the gum.

So why are the living sometimes confused with the dead? Often the physician or surgeon is to blame, for his lack of care. But there are other occasions when even the keenest will not detect a pulse, yet the pulse exists. There are times when the breath does not lift the ribs, nor mist a mirror, nor stir a feather, but the corpse is breathing still. I have heard that sometimes when people fall into deep water, deep water that is very cold, they may remain chill and extinguished for an hour or more, and yet the spark of life is flickering within them; when warmth returns to their organs, when it spreads to their limbs and their heart and their muscles gather strength—why, then they may sit up, and speak, to the horror and astonishment of the mourners.

This is what I have heard: although, unfortunately, I have had no opportunity of making actual experiments upon drowned persons.

The house is stone, a farmhouse, built on ground that is thin and poor. In his family, he is the tenth child, and the last. When there is no room at the fire, he is kicked out into the yard. Gradually, as he sees his siblings carried to the churchyard, room is made, but by then he is not accustomed to hearthside comforts, and the company of those who remain makes him uneasy.

At six years old he is sent out into the fields to pick stones, and also to scare crows. The crows watch him for any advantage. They circle in the air, talking about him in their intelligent voices. Sometimes he thinks they are plotting to take out his eyes.

Once your eyes are out you can't get a second pair. He pictures himself flipping on his back like a landed fish, his spine flexing and arcing, beating the ungiving ground with the flat of his palms. The first scream is practicing to come out of his mouth and the first stream of vomit. The crows have got his eyes in their beaks and are toddling over the ruts in the direction of East Kilbride.

There never was a man that wanted to be a great man ever was a great man. My present state of life I neither thought of nor could imagine. I am not a rich man, in fact I am poor, yet not poor in esteem; I say without boasting—pride not being in my nature—that the finest medical scholars of Europe have written me testimonials, and the most eminent surgeons in these islands and beyond crave for their sons a place at my table. And how, as the unmannerly Scots lad I am, could I have predicted this eminence?

While my brothers prospered at the academy, my school was the moor, hedge, and field. I asked questions to which few knew the answer and none cared to give it. Why do the leaves fall? Why do the birds sing? They would hit me across the ear and shove me out into the stark, away from the smell of humanity. In the end I preferred it so, I liked the keen wind against the smoky fug, my silent company against their chattering. My outdoor life, the labour to which I was born, hardened my hands and my spirit. I was thought of small account, and believed I was. My eyes followed the turning leaf, the bird in flight, the moon's phases.

. . .

His father, fifty when he was born and suffering with the gravel, frequently hit him across the ear. Mostly; whenever he saw him. This went on until he was thirteen, when his father died. By then he had acquired a high-shouldered look, and a habit of trying to see behind him.

four

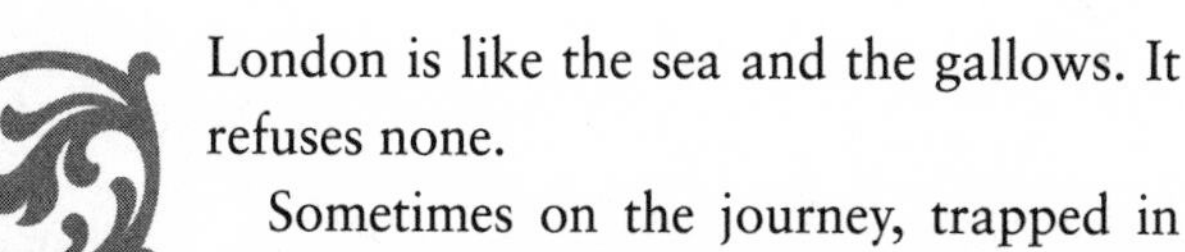

London is like the sea and the gallows. It refuses none.

Sometimes on the journey, trapped in the ship's stink and heave, they had talked about the premises they would have at journey's end. They should be commodious, Vance said, and in a fashionable neighbourhood, central and well-lit, on a broad thoroughfare where the carriages of the gentry can turn without difficulty.

"My brother has a lodging in St. Clement's Lane," Claffey said. "I don't know if it's commodious."

Vance blew out through his lips. "Nest of beggars," he said. "As to your perquisites and your embellishments, Charlie, they say a pagoda is the last word in fashion."

"A pagoda?" The Giant frowned. "I'd sooner a triumphal arch."

"Let's see when we get there," Vance said. "I think we'll call you Byrne, Charles Byrne. It's more select."

A lurch of the timbers, a fresh outswell of mould and fust; Jankin was sick—he had the knack and habit—on Claffey's feet. Claffey kicked out. Hot words flew in the stinking space.

"Will you have a story?" the Giant soothed them. For the time must be passed, must be passed.

"Go on," Vance said.

The Giant did not stop to ask what kind of story they would like, for they were contentious, like fretful children, and were in no position to know what was good for them. "One day," he began, "the son of the king of Ireland journeyed to the East to find a bride."

"Where East?" Vance asked. "East London?"

"Albania," the Giant said. "Or far Cathay."

"The Land of Nod," said Claffey, sneering. "The Kingdom of Cockaigne."

"Wipe yourself, stench-foot," O'Brien said, "then pin back your ears. Do you think I tell tales for the good of my soul?"

"Sorry," Claffey said.

"One day the son of the king of Ireland journeyed to the East to find a bride, and he hadn't gone far on his road when he met a short green man. The strange gentleman hailed him, saying—"

"I don't like a tale with a short green man in it," Jankin said.

The Giant turned to him, patient. "If you will wait a bit, Jankin, the short green man will grow as big as the side of a hill."

"Oh," Jankin said.

The wind moaned, the boards creaked and shifted beneath them. From the deck the world appeared no longer solid but a concatenated jumble of grey dots, sometimes defined and sometimes fusing at the margins, the waves white and rearing, the clouds blackening en masse, the horizon crowded with their blocky forms and their outlines unnatural, like the sides of unimaginable buildings, set storey on storey like the tower of Babel.

Conversing with the sailors—who cowered away from his bulk—the Giant found he had regained his command of the English language. One day, he thought, we will be making tales out of this. Our odyssey to the pith of London's heart, to undying fame and a heavy purse. Rancour will be forgotten, and the reek of our fear in this ship's dark hole. In those days Jankin will say, Do you remember, Claffey, when I was sick on your feet? And Claffey will clap him on the back, and say, Oh I do indeed.

And so at that time, after his father's death and he being fourteen, fifteen years of age, John Hunter was still in the fields largely, the business of sending him to school having met with scant success. Having come home from the field to drink a bowl of broth, he heard one day a beating at the door, the main door of the house at Long Calderwood, and himself going to open it and propping out the door frame, short for his age but sturdy, his sleeves rolled and his red hands hanging, and there's the carrier with some distressed bundle wrapped in a blanket. It's human.

His first thought was that the man had been asked to transport some sick pauper, who being now about to take his leave of this mortal world was not required, I'll thank you very much, to piss and shit his last in the cart, and so the fastidious tradesman was attempting to pass on his responsibilities and let some unsuspecting farmer's floor be soiled. "Get off with you, and go to the Devil!" he'd cried, his temper even then being very hot if he thought anyone had made a scheme to take advantage of him.

But then from within the bundle came a long, strangulated coughing, and after that the words "John, is that you, my brother John?"

His brow furrowing, John approached the cart, and pulled back the blanket where it obscured the man's face. And who should it be, but his own dear brother James. James, who had taken a degree in theology. James, that was a gentleman. James, that had gone to London to join brother Wullie, and become a medical man, and a man of means. See how far education gets you.

"Y'd best come in. Can ye step down?"

"I'll have your arm," James quavered. "Dear brother John."

Stout brother John. He half-lifted his relative from the cart. "Is there a good fire?" James begged to know. Through the cloth of his coat John felt the quake of his body, his jumping pulses. There was a nasty smell on his breath: rot. Dumped on a three-legged stool, James seemed hardly able to support himself upright. "What means this?" John enquired. "What brings you home in this condition, mon?"

"I am done for," James said. "I am worn out from the dissection room, the noxious emanations from the corpses, their poisoned fluids and exhalations, and the long hours your brother Wullie keeps. So jealous is he of his subjects, that he bade me sleep at night under the post-mortem table, lest one of his rivals should crack in at the windows and carry off the corpse."

"I see. So theft of corpses is an ever-present worry, is it?" John asked. He clasped his hands behind his back and looked down at his shivering brother. Well he remembered the day James left for London, sovereigns in his purse, felicitations ringing in his ears, and a new hat in a leather box completing his general air as a man of present prosperity and greater ambition. And now—the ribs were stoved in, the stomach collapsed. There were two red blotches on his cheeks—a sick parade of well-being. "It seems to me you have come back to die," John said. "All our family have a charnel disposition. Have you heard of a great man, called Sir William Harvey? He dissected his own relatives."

James raised his head. Hope shone in his face. "Have you formed an interest, brother John, in matters anatomical?"

"But only after they were dead." He turned aside, calling out to his sister Dorothea to come and view James. "You need not fear me," he said, under his breath.

Dorothea came, and made a great fuss and to-do, and boiled something nourishing for the invalid. Dolly never criticised or carped, and when he became a great man himself he would have her for his housekeeper, since all his other sisters were now residing in the churchyard under sod.

When they docked, and stood on dry land, Pybus fell about, and affected to be unable to walk except in the manner of a sailor, rolling and slowly riding upon the element he has made his own. Claffey grew impatient with the joke, and kicked him, saying, "That'll give you something to straggle for."

The Giant looked up, scanned the English sky. A few scudding clouds, the promise of sun breaking through. "God's same sky over us all," he said. But the voices were foreign, the shoving, shouting men, the tangles of rope and rigging, the salt and fish odours, and the buildings piled on buildings, one house atop another. They had boarded after dark, so now Pybus gaped, and pointed. "How do they—"

"They fly," Vance said shortly.

"Jesus," said Pybus. "Englishmen can fly? And the women also?"

"No," Vance said. "The women cannot fly. They remain on what is called the lower storey, or ground floor, where the men are able to join them as they please, or, when they sicken of their nagging chatter and wish to smoke a pipe of tobacco, they unfold the wings they keep under their greatcoats, and flutter up to what are called the upper storeys."

"That's a lie," Claffey said. "They must have a ladder."

The Giant gave Claffey a glance that expressed pleasure at his ingenuity. He was familiar himself with the principle of staircases, but in the lifetime of these young fellows there had been no great house within a day's march, where they might see the principle applied.

"Oh yes," Vance said, sarcastically. "Surely, they have a ladder. Take a look, Claffey—don't you see them swarming over the surface of the buildings?"

They looked, and did not. Glass windows caught the light, but the Giant's followers saw glinting, empty air, air a fist could pass through, that flesh could pass through and not be cut.

On the quayside, Jankin leapt in the air, pointing. He was swelling with excitement, bubbling at the mouth. The black man he had seen strolled calmly towards them. He wore a good broadcloth coat and a clean cravat, being, as he was, employed at the docks as a respectable and senior kind of clerk. He was young, his plum-bloom cheeks faintly scarred, his eyes mild.

Jankin danced in front of him. He gave a shriek, like one of the parakeets the Giant had heard of. His grubby hand shot up, massaging the man's face, rubbing in a circle to see would the colour come off. Jankin stared at his grey-white, seamed palm, and clawed out his fingers, then rubbed and rubbed again at the fleshy, flattened nose.

"Get down, dog," Joe Vance said. "The gentleman is as respectable as yourself."

The black man reached out, and took Jankin's forearm in his hand. Gently he removed it from himself, pressing it inexorably into Jankin's chest, as if he would fuse it with the ribs. His mild eyes were quite dead. His mouth twitched, but it did not speak. He passed on, his tread firm, over the cobbles and towards the city he now called home.

The Giant said, "People are staring at me."

Vance said, "Yes, they would. I should hope so. That is the general idea." He rubbed his hands together. "Sooner we get you indoors and housed, the better for us all. We don't want them gaping for free."

The Giant saw the parakeets, green and gold, flit and swoop in a hot tangle of deeper green, and heard the alarm shrieks from their beating throats, and felt rope cut into skin and smelled the sweet, burned, branded flesh.

He called out after the black man, "Poor soul, you have a brand on your body."

The man called back, "Shog off, freak."

The first night of their walk to London, they begged lodgings in a barn. Joe Vance parlayed with the farmer, and purchased from him some milk, some beer, and some nasty dried-up bread with green mould on it. Claffey became militant, and raised a doubt about Joe Vance's abilities. The Giant was forced to detain their attention with a long tale. He settled them among the straw, and turned his cheek to the alien breeze. They had come so far in thin rain, their heads down, purposefully observing as little as they could. London would be all wonder, Vance had said. They were disposed to believe it, and not notice anything immediate: just walk. They had expected lush valleys, mounts snow-topped, fountains, a crystal house or mansion at each turn in the road: but no, it was tramp, tramp, just tramp.

"Look now," the Giant said. "Shouldn't we have a conveyance, Vance? I'd have thought a coach would have been sent for me, or some sort of elegant chariot?"

Hm. Or possibly not. Vance seemed likely to break out into a rage, which he did too readily when things went wrong. "What kind of coach?" he yelled. "One with the roof cut off? Who's going to wreck a perfectly good coach for the onetime transport of a giant? It isn't as if England is teeming with giants, it isn't as if having made a ruin of a perfectly sound vehicle they can hire it out again on a weekly basis, is it? No Englishman does business that way!"

"What about a chariot?" the Giant asked mildly. "The same objection cannot be raised to a chariot."

"Oh yes, a chariot, but then it would have to be reinforced! You couldn't have your customer stepping in and putting his giant foot through it, so it would have to be strengthened—which costs money—and then drawn by heavy horses."

"Did you not think of this before?" Pybus asked. (And Pybus was only a boy.)

"Just what are you insinuating?" Joe Vance bellowed. "Are you insinuating that I have in some way exaggerated my experience as a giant's agent? Because if you are, Pybus, I'll slit your nostrils and pull your brains out through the opening, and then I'll pound them to a paste and put them down for rat poison."

The Giant asked, "Do you know the tale of the man that was drunk in the company of the priest, and the priest changed him to a mouse, and he got eat by his own cat?"

"No," Jankin said. "By God, let's have that tale!"

. . . As for what we can say of Buchanan—whoopsy-go Buchanan! Why John am I glad tae see ye—hup, whop, ye'll take a drop, take another, take a flask, woeful tangle wi ma feet, here's a go, here's to you, here's to lads, hup! Hic! Take a sip! Never mind, sit ye down, mind the chair, chink the cup, Saturday night, wife's a-bed, hic! Whop! Saints Alive!

Slithery-go, oh, hey, clattery-hic—oh, phlat, hold yer cup out, no harm done—what a daft bloody place to put a staircase!

Well, Buchanan was an episode, nothing more. The man was not untalented as a cabinet-maker, but he could not keep his books straight, nor would a coin lodge in his pocket for more than an hour before it would be clamouring to be out and into the pocket of some purveyor of wine and spirits. In those first days in Glasgow, in the house of the said Buchanan, he would grieve—on windy days, the notion of fields would possess him, the sigh of the plane under his hand would turn to the breeze's sough, and he would long to lie full length upon the earth, listening to the rocks making and arranging themselves, and deep in the soil the eternal machinations of the worms. But he said to himself, conquer this weak fancy, John Hunter, because fortunes are made in cities, and you must make yours. At night he opened the shutter, letting in the cold, watching the moon over the ridge tiles, and the stars through smoke.

Buchanan was a hopeless case. His slide to bankruptcy could not be checked. He had taught a skill, at least; now he, John Hunter, could say, "I am a man who can earn a living with my hands." But he was glad when he was able to pack his bundle and foot it back to Long Calderwood.

Buchanan died. Brother James died.

One day a letter came. "Wullie's sent for me," he said to Dorothea. "I've to go south. He's wanting a strong youth."

"Then I suppose you'll do," his sister said.

Seventeen forty-eight saw John Hunter, a set-jawed red-head astride a sway-backed plodder, heading south towards the stench of tanneries and soap-boilers. He came to London across Finchley Common, with the gibbetted corpses of villains groaning into the wind. A hard road and a stony one, with constant vigilance needed against the purse-takers, but he was counselled against the sea voyage by brother Wullie, who had once been in a storm so horrible that the ship's masts were almost smashed down, seasoned sailors turned white from terror, and a woman passenger lost her reason, and has not recovered it till this day.

At the top of Highgate Hill he came to the Gatehouse Tavern, and observed London laid out below him. The evening was fine and the air mild.

It was an undrained marsh, the air above it a soup of gloom. The clouds hung low, a strange white light behind them. The Giant and his companions picked their way among the stinking culverts, and hairless pigs, foraging, looked up to glare at them, a metropolitan ill-will shining red and plain in their tiny eyes. As they tramped, their feet sank in mud and shite, and the sky seemed to lower itself onto their shoulders. As night fell, they saw the dull glow of fire. Men and women, ragged and cold as hermits, huddled round the brick kilns, cooking their scraps of food. They squatted on their haunches, looking up bemused as O'Brien passed them. Their eyes were animal eyes, glinting. He thought they were measuring the meat on his bones. For the first time in his life he felt fear: not the holy fear a mystery brings, but a simple contraction in his gut. All of them—even Vance, even Claffey—stepped closer to his side.

"Keep walking," the Giant said. "An hour or two. Then lavish baths await us, and the attentions of houris and nymphs."

"And feather beds," said Jankin, "with quilts of swansdown. And silk cushions with tassels on."

London is ringed by fire, by ooze. Men with ladders carry pitch-soaked ropes in the streets, and branched globes of light sprout from the houses. Pybus thinks they have come to a country where they do not have a moon, but Vance is sure they will see it presently, and so they do, drowned in a muddy puddle in Chandos Street.

❦

John's arrival was well-timed, for it was two weeks before the opening of brother Wullie's winter lecture programme. "I hear you're good with your hands," Wullie said.

He grunted: "Who says so?"

"Sister Dorothea."

Wullie put his own hands together. He had narrow white gentleman's hands. You would never know, to look at them, where they ventured: the hot velvet passages of London ladies who are enceinte, and the rigid bowels of dishonourable corpses.

Wullie had also a narrow white gentleman's face, chronically disappointed. It was some four years since his fiancée Martha died, and he had not found either inclination or opportunity to court any other woman; pale-eyed chastity had him in her grasp, and he thought only of sacrifice, late hours, chill stone rooms that keep the bodies fresh. The rooms of his mind were cold like this, and it was difficult to imagine him sighing and groaning, all night on a feather mattress beside the living Martha with her juices and her pulses, her dimples and her sighs and her "yes Wullie, yes Wullie, oh yes just there Wullie, oh my little sweetheart, can you do it over again?" Easier to imagine him a-bed with the dead woman, four years buried and dried to bone.

Easy to see, Wullie creeping up from the foot of the bed, his tongue out, daintily raising the rotted shroud: fingering her phalanges with a murmur of appreciation, creeping each pointed finger over the metatarsals and tarsals while his nightshirt, white as a corpse, rolls up about his ribs. It's with a gourmet's desire he sighs; then tibia and fibula, patella, and—ah, how he smacks his dainty lips, as he glides up the smooth femur, towards his goal! He pants a little, crouching over her, scarred Scottish knees splayed—and now he probes, with expert digit, the frigid cavity of her pelvis.

"Are you quite well, brother John?" Wullie asked.

"Aye. Oh, aye."

"You are not fevered?"

"Only deep in thought."

"Then fall to work on these arms. I am told you are observant and deft. Let us try your vaunted capacities."

The arms came wrapped in cloths, bloodless like wax arms, but they were not wax. Severed at the shoulder; and his job to dissect, to make preparations, to serve the students with a feast for their eyes. His voice quivered. "Whose are they?"

"Whose?" The little query dripped with ice.

"Two arms—I mean, a right and a left—are they from the same man? I mean, is he dead, or was he in an accident?"

He was a raw boy, after all. He'd done little but stone the crows, follow the plough. Glasgow had been an intermission, and had not taught him about men with no arms.

Wullie said, "When I was a student in France, there was none of this nonsense of forty men crowding round the dissecting table, craning their necks and babbling. To each Frenchman, there was one corpse, and in the dissecting chamber there was an aura of studious calm. The French are a frivolous nation, and deeply mistaken in many of their inclinations, but in this vital matter they have the right of it."

John got to work dissecting the arms. Later, he castigated himself for a jimmy idiot—bursting out like that in front of Wullie, as if it should matter where limbs came from. Still, he couldn't help wondering, speculating in his mind: making up a life to fit the possessor of the fibrous, drained muscle. It was matter, no impulse to drive it; only half its nature was on display, structure but not function, and he knew this was less than half the truth, for how can you understand a man if you don't see him in action? He couldn't help thinking of Martha, when he himself lay down at night: he saw her narrow and flat and yellow-white against the bedlinen, and Wullie puffing above her, his shirt scooped up, and he heard the little chattering cries of pleasure escaping her nonexistent lips.

"Slig!" said Joe Vance. "Hearty Slig!"

They were standing in some alley. Vance clapped the man on the shoulder. His head indicated a low door, half-open, from which the man had just emerged: behind him, steps running down into the earth. "Can you lodge us?" Vance asked. "One night only. Tomorrow we move on to greater things."

Slig gnawed his lip. "Two pennies each," he said.

"Slig! And yourself an old friend of mine!"

"Be reasonable. I have to cover the cost of the straw. And fourpence for the big fella. I shall have to turn two away if I'm to let him in."

"But it's a privilege to have him under your roof! Besides being huge, he can tell tales and make prophecies."

"Fourpence," Slig said. "Liquor's extra."

Sighing, Vance disbursed the coins. Pybus and Claffey were heroes about the steps, striding down into the cellar as if they had been doing steps all their lives—though there was a moment of nervous hesitation from Claffey at the top of the flight, and the manner in which his frown changed to a cocky grin showed that he had harboured some anxiety. Jankin could not be persuaded to put his first foot forward, even though Pybus ran up and then down again to show how easy it was: eventually, the Giant had to carry him.

The room was low and filled with smoke. There was straw underfoot, and men and women sitting, convivial, their pots in their hands, and nobody drunk yet; rushlight on exiles' faces, the sound of a familiar tongue. And a grubbing sound from the shadows, a snorting.

"Jesus," Jankin said. "We have touched down among the rich. These fellows have got a pig."

There was a moment's silence, while the people considered the

Giant; an intake of breath, and then applause rang to the roof. Men and women stood up and cheered him. "One boy of ours," a woman said. "The true type." She stretched up, and kissed his hip. "Giants are extinct here for hundreds of years."

"And why is this?" the Giant asked; for the woman, who was not young, had a look of some intelligence, and the matter puzzled him.

She shrugged, and with a gesture of her small fingers pulled her kerchief down, modest, hiding her rust-red curls. "It may be that they were shut up and starved, or hunted with large dogs. The Englishman craves novelty, as long as it will pack and decamp by the end of the week. He does not like his peace disturbed; it is the English peace, and he thinks it is sacred. He magnifies his own qualities, and does not like anyone to be bigger than himself."

"This bodes ill for my projected fame and fortune," the Giant said.

"Oh, no! Your keeper was right enough to bring you. You will be the sensation of a season."

"At the end of which, I shall still be tall."

"But I expect you can tell stories? Giants usually can. Even the English like stories—well, some stories anyway. The ones where they win."

"This is not what we were promised," Claffey said. He looked around. "Here, Joe Vance! This is not what we were promised! But for the breath of the mountain air, we might be back at Connor's."

"No, Vance," the Giant said. "It's not what I'd call commodious."

"Contain yourself in patience," Vance said. "Give me the chance, will you, of a day to prospect for some premises for us."

"I'd have thought you'd got it already fixed," Claffey said. "That's what it means, being an agent, doesn't it?"

"Being an agent is an art you will never acquire, bog-head."

"Now, Vance," said the Giant. "Temperate yourself."

"If you don't like it, you know what you can do," Vance said.

"Claffey, have patience," Pybus said. "Joe will get us a place tomorrow. One with a pagoda."

"Did we agree on a pagoda?" the Giant said. "I still favour a triumphal arch."

"A triumphal arch is timeless good taste," said a man squatting at their feet.

"Whereas a pagoda, it's a frivolity worn out within the week."

"It's right," said the red-headed woman. "There's a whiff of the vulgar about a pagoda."

Vance spread out his hands, smiling now. "Good people! He's a giant! I'm a showman! Don't say vulgar! Say topical! Say it's all the buzz!"

"Tell that giant to sit down," said an old man, who was leaning against the wall. "He is disturbing the air."

"He is blind," said the squatting man, nodding towards the speaker. "Strange vibrations bother him."

The Giant folded himself stiffly, and sat down in the straw. Pybus bounced down beside him. Jankin was admiring the pig. Joe Vance looked easy. Claffey looked peevish.

"We saw pigs on our way," Jankin said. "Skinny brutes. Not a one that could hold a candle to this. Why, at home, he'd be the admiration of a parish."

"All of us own this pig," the blind man said. "He is our great hope."

A young girl with an open face, slightly freckled across the nose, reached up and plucked at the Giant's sleeve. "Would you oblige, and cheer us now with an anecdote? We are, all of us, far from home."

"Very well," said the Giant. He looked at Claffey, at Pybus, at Joe Vance. He stretched out his legs in front of him; then, seeing he was taking too much floor space, drew them up again. "Here's one you'll know or not, and you may make your comments as if we were at home and gathered at Connor's."

He thought: there's only this earth, after all. The ground beneath us and God's sky above, and we will get used to this, because people can get used to anything, and giants can too.

The young girl looked down, smiling in pleasure. She had long fair hair, almost white even in the cellar fug: like a light underground, O'Brien thought, Persephone's torch made from a living head. The girl's cheeks were pink and full; she had eaten only yesterday. She settled her hair about her, combing it with her fingers, arranging it about her shoulders, drawing it across her face like a curtain. And now the outline of bowed shoulders, of sharp faces, must be blurred for her, and the facts of life softened: like a slaughter seen through gossamer, or a throat cut behind a fan of silk.

"A year or two ago," said the Giant, "there was a young woman, pretty and light of foot, walking the road alone at night, coming to her cousin in Galway, with her babby of scarce six months laid to her breast. She had been walking for many a mile, walking through a dense wood, when—"

"A demon comes up and eats her," said Pybus, with confidence.

"—she emerged at a crossroad," the Giant continued, "just as the moon rose above the bleak and lonely hills. She stood there bedazzled, in the moonlight, wondering, which way shall I go? She looked down, into the face of her babby, but snug in his sling he was asleep and dreaming, dreaming of better times, and she could get no direction there. Shall I, she thought, linger here till morning, making my bed in the mossy ditch, as I have done many times before? It may be that in the morning some knowledgeable traveller will come along, and direct my way, or perhaps even in my dream I will receive some indication of the shortest route to my cousin's house. I need hardly add, that her hair was long and curling and pale, her form erect, her body low and small but seemly, so that if the most vicious and ungodly man had chanced to glimpse her he would have thought her one of the gentry, and would have crossed himself and left her unmolested. Now this was her protection, as she walked the road, and she knew it; what man would touch a fairy, with a fairy babby bound in a cloth? And yet she was a mortal woman, with all her perplexities sitting heavy on her shoulders, and her worries making the weight of the babby increase with every mile she trod."

A man said, from the shadows, "I've heard of a type of fairy where they carry their babbies on their backs, and the nursing mothers have tits so long and supple that they can fling one over their shoulder so the babby can suck on it, which is a great convenience to them when they're labouring in the fields."

"Yes, well, some people will believe anything," the Giant said.

"Must be foreign," said a woman. "A foreign type. I've never heard it. Still and all, it would leave your hands free."

A man said, "Whoever heard of gentlefolk that labour in the fields?"

"Will you be quiet, down at the back?" Vance asked testily. "I've brought you over a master storyteller of unrivalled stature, and you're just about going the right way to irritate him, and then you'll be sorry, because he'll stamp on your heads and burst your bloody skulls."

"It's not worrying me, Joe," the Giant said. "Calm yourself and sit down, why don't you. Shall I go on?" There were murmurs of assent. "So: just then, as she was casting around, she heard a noise, and it was not the sound of a horse, and it was not very distant, and she discerned it was the slap of shoe-leather, and she thought, here is a man on the road who is either rich or holy, either merchant or priest, and I will beg either a blessing or a penny—who knows which will do me more good, in the long run?

"Then out of the shadows stepped a little man, with a red woollen cap upon his head, and carrying a leather bag. So he greeted her, and 'Step along with me,' he says, 'and I'll fetch you to a place you can sleep the night.' Now she looked at him with some dismay, for he was neither merchant nor priest, and she did not know what he was, or what he had in his leather bag. She says, 'The wind is fresh and the moon is high, and I think I'll step out, because my relatives are gathered about their hearth in the town of Galway, and they are waiting for me.'

"And he says to her, very low and respectful, 'Mistress, will you walk with me for all that? I will bring you to a hall where a little babby is crying with hunger, with no one to feed him; because his mother is dead and we have no wet nurse amongst us. Do me this favour,' he says, 'as I observe your own child is plump and rosy, and he will not miss the milk, but without it our babby will die. And if you will do me this favour, I will give you a gold piece from my leather bag.'

"And then he gave the bag a good shake, and she could hear the chink of gold pieces from within."

"She ought not go, for all that," the red-haired woman observed. "It will end badly."

"And aren't you the shrivelled old bitch!" Pybus said. "Not go, and have the babby starve?"

"I'm telling you," the woman said. "Just wait, you'll see."

"Do you know this story, then?" Pybus asked her.

"No, but I know that type of man that wears a red woollen cap."

"Well now," the Giant said, "let the true facts of what occurred put an end to your debate. For she was an amiable, good-hearted young woman, and she says to him, 'For such a pitiful tale as you have told me I'll come to the babby, and ask you no money, for you are an old man, and you may need your cash yourself, by and by.' "

"Oh, Jesus!" Joe Vance said. "If that were my wife, I'd beat her into better sense."

"So off they step together, many a mile, turning her out of her true path, and still her babby sleeps, until she grows footsore and says to the old man, 'I fear we will not be there by morning.'

" 'We shall come to the place before dawn, I promise you,' says the old man. 'This is a king's son I am taking you to nurse, and it is not likely I should find him lying under the next hedge.' "

"A pox on kings," said the blind man. "What do kings avail? Better he dies."

"You speak out of your bitterness and affliction," the Giant said. "Not all kings are bad."

"Yes," said the blind man. "They are bad inherently. It is not a question of their personal character. Kingship is an institution merely silly in itself, and pernicious as well."

"Less politics," the fair young woman said. "I want to hear of the girl, she is feeling she can't go a step more, so what is the old man going to do to coax her, as she doesn't seem to want his money?"

"Put his hand up her skirts and wiggle his finger?" Vance asked. "That's often known to invigorate a female."

The red-head yawned. "Little man, you might wave your cock to the five points," she said. "Not a woman in Ireland but would be laughing."

"Go on," Pybus said, impatient. "Go on with the tale, Charlie."

The Giant began again, taking up the young woman's voice. " 'Good sir, I did not know it was a king's son you were bringing me to.' So off they step, across field and stream, for what seems another hour, and another, and another, and dawn does not break, nor does the sky lighten one crack, and on and on they go, into the dark. And again she is weary, the babby grown a leaden weight, her feet cold and sore, her breath coming short and painful, and every limb crying out for rest and warmth, her belly rumbling too. She says, 'King's son or no, I can walk no more.'

"Then the old man takes from under his coat a silver flask, and hands it to her, and she marvels at its workmanship, for it was finer than any she had ever seen or dreamed of. 'Take a draught!' says he, and she takes a draught, and it is like nothing she has ever tasted in her mortal life. It is like honey but sweeter, it is like new milk but milder, it is like wine but it is stronger than any wine that was ever poured into a chalice. And as soon as she drinks it down, she feels all weariness drop away from her, and all torment of mind, and the babby is as light as air, and her feet feel as if she's on her way to a dance, twitching at the first strain of the fiddle and ready to jig through the night. So she says to the old man, 'With a draught like that I could walk for half a year.' "

"Hm," said the red-head. "You notice how he only offered it after she said she was all through and done for? Why didn't he give her a swig when he met her? Too mean, that's what."

"Presently," the Giant said, "they came to a halt. Before them was a forest."

"I knew a forest would be in it," Jankin said. "There is a demon in that forest, I bet you."

"Seal your gawpy mouth, mush-head," Joe Vance said. "Go talk to your friend the pig."

The Giant glanced at Joe; he saw he was heart and soul in the tale. He's not a bad man at that, he thought, and he's a good standby when the weapon of words must be employed; with his natural, flowing abuse, he's working within a fertile tradition. "She enters the forest," he said. "They walk a half-mile. She's light now, her steps bouncing. Before her, she can see nothing but trees. Then when she looks again, she can see a gate set into the trees—and the gate is made of gold."

"A common delusion," said the red-head.

"Then the old man says, 'Mistress, will you enter in?' She does so. And there she beholds such splendour as there never was this side of heaven."

"Silk cushions with tassels is in it," Jankin said.

"Indeed," said the Giant. He closed his eyes, and drew in his brows. So many times he had been called upon to describe splendour, and so many times he had called upon himself to do it; by now the thread of his invention was wearing thin. "There were hangings on the wall," he began, "rich and dense tapestries, with every manner of flower and child and beast depicted upon them.

There were mirrors between these hangings, their gilt frames studded with rubies. There were candles blazing, and the skins of lions to sit on, and there was a huge joint of meat roasting on a spit, and a mastiff—no, a brace of mastiffs—to turn it. So when she sees all this, she thinks, I should have taken that gold piece after all, because it's obvious now that there's plenty more where that came from."

"First glimpse of sense she's shown all evening," Claffey said.

"So there she stood, her babby in her arms, looking about her open-mouthed. At one end of the great room a door opened, and in came a man and a woman, tall and elegant, attired in sumptuous robes embroidered with silk. She bobbed her head then, and she was shy and tongue-tied, having no acquaintance until now with princes, which was what she took them to be. But they spoke her very fair—their voices were low and gracious, a whisper merely—and stretching out their hands to her they drew her towards them, and said they would conduct her to where the child was. So they took her into another great chamber, its hangings even richer than the first, the logs blazing, and golden birds singing in their cages, and the music of a harp sounding in her ears as sweet as the breath of angels. Surely I've died and gone to heaven, she said to herself—but then the woman reached forward to her, and drew her babby out of her arms, and the man put a hand on her breast and, with the utmost reverence, uncovered her dug. 'Here,' says the woman, and led her to the cradle, which was draped in purple velvet and set on a stand carved of ivory, fetched from—"

"Jesus!" Claffey said. "I am getting weary of the catalogue of furnishings, so I am. A hand plucks back the curtain and she sees—"

"—a yellow-skinned babby, its skin wrinkled, its eyes rheumy—"

"Much like he must have been," the red-head said, indicating Vance.

"—so ugly she had never seen a child like it, and her gorge rose, and she said—putting aside all common politeness, such was the strength of her feeling—I don't know that I can touch it. Then the man and woman again spoke to her, and their voices were low and whispering and they seemed to hold in them the same shivering note of the harp-string and the melody of the golden birds bowing on their perch—and they said, cooing to her, 'There's nothing the matter with the child, except want of nourishment.'

"And the woman shook her head, saying, 'If that's the manner and appearance of a king's son, my own fair child should be emperor of the earth and skies.' But she pitied them, and she pitied the yellow baby, and so she lifted it from the cradle of velvet and ivory, and laid it to her blue-veined breast. And all the while her own child lay sleeping in the arms of the woman so richly dressed, and lay so quiet and still that it seemed he was under an enchantment."

"Which indeed he was," the red-haired woman said. Again she plucked nervously at her kerchief. "You could see it coming a mile off."

"I wish you'd be quiet, mother," Pybus said.

"Yes." Jankin broke off from his play with the pig. "I want to hear, I want to hear. It is not the demon tale we thought it was."

A man laughed. "They are simple, these. Come over the water just now."

But the blind man shushed him, saying severely, "It is seldom, in these debased days, we are able to hear a tale told in the antique fashion, by a gent of such proportions."

"So when the yellow child was laid to her breast, he took a fierce hold, and drank greedily, and she cried out, 'Oh, you did not say he had teeth! Surely, blood is springing from my tit!' "

"Dear, dear," Vance said satirically. "What the female sex have to endure!"

" 'Ah, my dear, he has but one tooth, one tooth only,' said the queen, soothing her. 'He will suck me dry!' the young woman cried. 'Feed him but one minute longer,' they coaxed, 'and then you shall have a soft bed to lie in all night, and a goosedown quilt to cover you, and in the morning we will give you seven gold pieces, and shoes to your feet, and in no time at all you will be in Galway amongst your own people.'

"So, thinking of the bed, and the quilt, and the shoes, and the gold, she let the yellow child drain her. The moment it was done, it flinched away its head, like a rich man offered a dry crust. And the queen took it from her—and all at once, she felt her eyelids droop, her legs weaken—and that was the last thing she knew."

"Now you will hear the coda," said the red-head. "I feel I could whistle it. It is no pretty tune."

"Morning came at last. She woke, and put out her hand to stroke the feather bed—"

"But felt," said the blind man, "only a mulch of leaves."

"It was cold, and the harp-string was mute, and only a common sparrow of the hedgerows sang in her ear. She opened her eyes, sat up, looked around her—and the hand that had smoothed the bed grasped a handful of weeds, too rank to feed a cow—"

"And her babby?" the freckled girl said. Her fingers parted her curtain of hair. Her voice was sharp with anxiety.

"She is twelve years old," the red-head said. "Excuse her. She has not heard many tales."

The Giant shook his head. "Then this is a sad one, for a beginner. For the young lady, who last night was in the hall of kings—now her feet are in the ditch, her mouth is dry, there is muck in her hair, and her belly is empty. And she cries, 'My babby! Where is he?' She casts around, but her rosy babby is not to be seen—and then from the hedge she hears a little bleat—"

The red-head laughed. "Time to run."

"—and looking into the hedge what should she find but the yellow child, its skin flapping, its eyes running and its nose snuffling, its evil pointed teeth grinning at her, and its wizened arms held out to fasten about her neck."

"Well?" asked a woman in the shadows. "Did she turn and walk away?"

"I think not," the red-head said. "It's the hand you're dealt, isn't it? She'd pick him up. It's what women do. She was a fool, and well-intentioned, and just a little bit greedy, and isn't that like most of us?"

Jankin gaped. "What happened to her babby? Did she get him back?"

"He was never seen again," the Giant said emphatically.

There was a long silence.

Jankin broke it. "Do you know what I think? I think, if she had not made the remark about the child's ill-looks, and not said that about her own child being an emperor, I think they might well have seen her safe back on the road and a penny in her hand. For they are decent-minded people on the whole, the gentry, but they will not stand for spitefulness."

"In my opinion," said the red-head, "when the old man first offered her a gold piece, she should have said, 'Show us the colour of it,' then grabbed it in her hand and run."

"Well, however it may be, and however you think," said the Giant, "this happened to my own cousin, on the road to Galway, but one or two years back. And this is the story, as I had it from her own lips; and if you don't like it, you may lengthen it by your complaints."

There came from the company a great sigh, an exhalation; they were, on the whole, satisfied. Drink had now been taken, and Slig came down the steps with a cannikin, offering more. The cellar was warming up, with the press of extra people, and the heat of the pig, and the heat of contentious opinion. The blind man had sunk down against the wall, into a heap of rags, and he held out his beaker, his voice searching, "Slig? Slig? Fill us up here." He turned his face in the Giant's direction. "Would you like to hear our ballad, big man?"

"Certainly, yes."

"It is still in the making."

"That is the most interesting stage."

"So polite you are!"

"I add it to the advantages of nature."

"You do well." The blind man paused. "We are making a ballad about the circumstances in which we find ourselves. Does that suit you?"

"There was in former times a great poet who made verses upon the subject of the shovel he used to dig a road for Englishmen—so simple and pure his heart, and that object not too low. Can I then disdain your cellar, or the circumstances in which you are found?"

The blind man nodded. "So. Very well. I will proceed. We are making our ballad on Hannah Dagoe, a wild girl, that when the hangman came to noose her she knocked him clean out of the cart."

"What was her crime?" asked the Giant.

"Stealing a watch only, and that on St. Patrick's Day. She came out of Dublin, and her trade was milliner."

"Whenabouts was this?"

"I don't know. Some year. They hanged her, anyway. We have also a ballad of Thomas Tobin and William Harper, how William Harper was rescued from the Westminster Gatehouse by twenty Irish boys with cutlasses."

"And Thomas Tobin?"

"And how Thomas Tobin was not."

"Did they hang him?"

"I expect so. For Robert Hayes was hanged, though he spoke Latin like the pope. And Patrick Brown was hanged for stealing silver spurs. Bryan Cooley was hanged, and his wife and four of his children came from Ireland to see it. Patrick Kelly was hanged, that was fifty years old, that filed coins, that made a speech about if each had their own no man would be poor. James Carter was hanged, him that was five years with the French armies, and John Maloney, that fought in Sicily, which is a hot country at a good distance but it's not the Indies. John Norton was hanged, and him twelve years a soldier. Thomas Dwyer was hanged, that came from Tipperary and had no coat to his back. William Rine and James Ryan, Gerald Farrell and James Falconer, they were all turned off together. Teddy Brian was hanged and Henry Smith, that robbed the high bailiff of his gold-topped cane. Katherine Lineham was hanged, but her husband was hanged before her, and Ruggetty Madge was hanged, that was Katherine Lineham's friend, and Redman Keogh, and black and damned Macdonnel that sold them all to save his neck, but they hanged him anyway. William Bruce was hanged, that stole a silk kerchief and a man's wig off his head, and they found him in a barn, he was a man out of Armagh. James Field was hanged, him that was a boxer, and the watch were afraid of him till they came to take him in strength. Joseph Dowdell was hanged, he was a Wicklow man but fell to picking pockets in Covent's Garden. Garret Lawler was hanged, that was a cardsharp. Thomas Quinn was hanged, and Alexander Byrne, and Dan the Baker, and Richard Holland, and all of those you could find any fine night of the year drinking at the Fox Tavern in Drury Lane. Patrick Dempsey was hanged, he was a sailor, turned off when he was drunk. William Fleming was hanged, he was a highwayman. Ann Berry was hanged, a weaver turned a rough robber, and Margaret Watson, she heeded no laws. Robert Bird was hanged, and of him I know not a jot that would make a line or half of one. James Murphy and James Duggan were hanged, and their bodies cut up by the surgeons."

"Dear God," said the Giant. "Was the whole country of Ireland hanged, and not one spared?"

"When the people gather they call it the crack-neck assembly. When you are turned off they call it the cramp-jaw, and the new jig without music, and dancing in the sheriff's picture frame."

"It is the slaughter of a nation," the Giant said.

"Katherine Lineham was what we call a hemp-widow. Her husband was a month in Newgate, and she so in love with him that every day she waited till she saw him led from the cell to the chapel, that she might see his shadow slide against the wall. Oh, then how he did bounce, his face to the city! *Rope* is the first word of English that an Irishwoman learns. *Hang* is the word of her husband: hang him, the thief, he is a rebel, hang him for a rogue. *Dog* is the word of her children: kick them out, kick them out like dogs. These are the next words: *papist,* and *starve him,* and *let him be whipped.*"

They separated then; the women moving chastely to one side of the hovel, the men to the other. A low hum of good-nights, smiles in the dark. By the last flicker of light the Giant saw the red-headed woman draw the fair young girl to her breast, patting her, and he heard the tiny bleatings of sorrow and loss suppressed. Later, when the darkness was thick and clotted and absolute, he heard Claffey and Joe Vance whispering to each other. "I for one don't believe it. Because, lion skins? He said she saw them, heaped in the great chamber. How would they get lion skins? How would they get lion skins, in Ireland?"

"Also," Claffey said, "it couldn't have happened to his cousin. He wouldn't be able to have a cousin that was low and small. Any cousin of his would be a monster like he is."

I have a difficulty myself, the Giant thought. The fine workmanship of the flask: how did she see it in the dark?

Through her fingertips? That's possible.

Jankin and Pybus lay on their sides in the straw, heads down and knees drawn up. Both of them cried in their sleep.

"Sir, let me tell you, the noblest prospect which a Scotchman ever sees, is the high road that leads him to England." It's true. True. Buchanan, all that giggle and tripe—it's behind him.

Long Calderwood's behind him now: the thatch, the tending of the graves, pulling up weeds when ye could be doing something more useful. Beginning as Wullie's gofer, sleeping on the floor at Hatton Garden (we all, my dear brother John, must endure these preliminaries), he became a trusted manager in Wullie's deeper designs (to each Englishman, one corpse) and in summer attended upon Cheselden as he committed surgery against the patients at Chelsea Hospital, while in the winter he served as dissector and factotum to Wullie again, who was then pursuing his increasingly celebrated series of lectures in anatomy. A year later he was a surgical student at Barts, and a year after that he moved with Wullie to Jermyn Street, and fetched down sister Dolly, who had been left alone at Long Calderwood with the weeding. Wullie—always carping, criticising, and finding fault—came to him one day and told him to proceed to Oxford, to obtain a seemly education: "For your uncouth manners, John, hamper the family, and my nerves are frayed with anticipating what you will say and do next. And at the venerable seat of learning they will inculcate that knowledge of the great civilisations of Greece and Rome which seems to have escaped you, and they will instil merely by example, shall we say, a more urbane demeanour, a lighter touch, a wittier—oh well no, perhaps not." Wullie turned away. "We must be realistic in our expectations, must we not? But try, brother John; do make a little curtsey in gentility's direction. You are too much the North Briton still."

John thought: I see you every night in your bed, fockin a skeleton.

At Oxford he lasted all of two months, and he made sure that, even at two months, he outstayed his welcome. He cracked Wullie's scheme like a louse; what, make a canting professor of him? All he knows, all he needs to know, he feels under his hands, or through the knife's blade. Flesh and steel; they are their own encyclopedia.

Yet did they not give him a post at St. Georges' Hospital, and a little house to go with it? Later, St. Georges' elected him a governor, but by now he was possessed by a great interest in gunshot wounds, an interest that he found hard to indulge, so near to Hyde Park. It was a defect, in Londoners, that they did not shoot each other enough. "Why, why, why," he asked (his face reddening, blood thudding through his system, ker-clunk, ker-clunk, ker-clunk), "why do you insist on treating a gunshot wound as different from any other?" "Because it is," was all they could say. Because it is. Because it is, because we believe it is. Exasperation drove him to the post of army surgeon. William flared his nostrils. "A step retrograde, I'd have thought?" Wullie by now had got his dainty fingers up to the wrist in the cunt of the queen of England, who was puffing and squeezing out of her innards a prince of Wales.

But later John was able to publish a treatise on gunshot wounds, which owed nothing to Wullie at all, and brought him the wholehearted esteem of the profession. In the year 1767, he was elected a fellow of the Royal Society, an honour which came to him a full three months before it came to his brother. In that same year, while dancing—an understandable reaction to good news, though a rare one, for him—he snapped his Achilles tendon. ("Really, John—what Hibernian romp was this?") Another St. Georges' appointment put some money in his account, and by the time Wullie vacated Jermyn Street and he took over the lease he had surgeon-apprentices bound to him at five hundred guineas for their five years, and live-in students who paid a hundred per annum for their board—surprising, when it comes to it, what a student can bring in when it's one hundred pounds minus cost of porridge, meat but sparingly, linen-wash extra, and always use yesterday's milk.

In 1771 he published a first part of his treatise on the teeth—his knowledge, again, thanks to his presence on the battlefield, because the dead don't squeal and scream when their teeth are drawn, and in order to write in this speciality what do you need? Teeth, teeth, a plentiful amount of teeth! That year also he got married to Anne, the daughter of Robert Boyne Hume, a surgeon of repute who had helped him in his career. It was ten years since he had met her father, and it was true he had dallied, after his initial proposal, but women cost so! Lace and musical evenings, the scraps for covering screens and what-all, minced chicken-liver for lapdogs, and accoutrements for their heads! It is Anne's fancy—and she had one of her relatives execute it—to paint a gallimaufry of cupids on the panels of their bedroom wall; there they bob and gambol, in and out of season, bare pink flesh bubbling and seething among the fair-weather clouds.

Since 1780, Wullie and John are no longer on speaking terms. They have quarrelled about the structure of the placenta.

So raise a glass. Here's a toast to London, where the Hunters live and thrive, and where their prey survive as tripe-makers, spinners of catgut, coal-heavers and vinegar-brewers, industrious pencil-makers and ballad-singers, soap-boilers and cobblers, drovers and match-sellers and dealers in old clothes, where cobblers sleep under their stalls and milk-walkers in the cellar with the cow, where the cow is dying from lack of light and air, where the people are dying of dropsy, quinsy, tisick, measles, croup, gout, canker, teething, overlaying, mold-shot head, thrush, cough, whooping-cough, duelling, surfeit, pleurisy, dysentery, lethargy, child-bed, king's evil, and unknown causes: and some from grief, and some from a footpad's ball, some double-ironed in dungeons and some from the bite of a mad dog, some from French pox, cholic, gripes, flux, scurvy, fistula, worms: and are buried at St. Andrew above Bars and St. George the Martyr, at St. Saviour,

Southwark, and St. Paul Shadwell, at St. Giles without Cripple-gate and St. Botolph without Aldgate.

Joe Vance was visibly cheered when daylight came. “It’s just as the people said last night,” Slig told him. “They’re crying out for giants. They’re also extremely keen on two-headed calves, so if you have—”

“One wonder at a time,” Vance said. He turned to O’Brien. “I have made up my mind on it. We *will* call you Byrne, Charles Byrne. It meets with the approval of all here.” He tried it out. “Charles Byrne, the Surprising Irish Giant. The Tallest Man in the World.”

five

"Gentlemen, you will recall that my experience in this matter reaches back some thirty years, ever since, a young lad fresh from the farm, I was charged by my illustrious brother William to bring him the suitable and neccesary materials for his great work. And you will know that I stand before you not as some sniggling schoolmaster with his text and rule, but as an honest man like yourselves, who has digged and delved and dirtied his hands."

Fresh from the farm. John Hunter looks about him, at their blackguards' faces. It is night, and the room is chilly, so they sit muffled in the clothes they will wear when out and about. He has shown them his stock, and watched their faces for signs of levity and mirth on the one hand, or sickening on the other. Neither will do for him. Getting corpses is not for the queasy. It is not a sport either and yet . . .

"Those years are behind him, you'll say. He is grizzled now and bowed, not fleet as formerly, his hearing not so sharp; fitter for the laboratory, you'll say, and the lecture room. And yet there are nights . . . there are some black nights when I find myself restless, and I would wish to be out again with a swift and sober crew, with our dark lantern and our wooden shovels, our cords and sacks and crowbars."

Select your tools carefully . . .

Wooden shovels make no sound. (Grunts of effort, even, must be suppressed.) A stout canvas is needed to receive the earth. The hole is made at the head's end. The hooks, the crowbars, are to insert under the coffin lid. The earth at the foot acts as a counter-weight, so—breath indrawn, and held—the lid snaps across. With experience, it is possible to predict—with a thrill that runs from the palms to the elbows—the very second when the wood will crack.

The corpse then is roped beneath the arms, and hauled out, head first, like a difficult birth. Flapped onto dry land, it is straightened and stripped. The grave clothes are thrown back. The gaping sacks are drawn over the flesh, the knees pulled up, the head forced down, the whole returned—as if after birth comes conception—to that economical package in which we spend our nine months in the womb. And lashed with cords. A compact bundle: looking no bigger than a dog, or a few pounds of jostling turnips.

"You will need ladders, of course, to scale the cemetery walls. May I advise you that a rope ladder is more discreet? Yet even then, if stopped in the street with it, you will find questions are asked, and so I advise you that a sexton with a well-oiled palm is more discreet still. Cultivate such men. Drink with them. Get to know their habits and their cant. Sympathise with them in the trials of their trade. Ask after their wife and babies. But when I say drink with them, I mean in your own time. Never take strong drink on a night when you mean to exercise your profession. You will do very well in this trade if you keep sober. The chief reason of bungling is strong drink.

"You will need a table showing the phases of the moon. This I will provide.

"Listen out for passing bells. Frequent ale-houses and listen for gossip of the lately dead. Make fast friends with the women who lay out corpses. A half-penny or a little love-talk may procure you access, and a chance to inspect. What are you looking for? I will come to that.

"If any stranger is weeping in the street, it is worth a moment of your time to approach him and tenderly ask why. If bereavement is the cause, then softly enquire, 'And where is your loved one laid out? And died of what cause? Just yesterday, you say? My, how I pity you, sir.'

"In grief, even strong men blurt, and this blurting may produce much valuable information.

"Have any of you a large number of lady friends?" He casts his eyes around the band. They manifest—could it be shock? Indignation? But he has given this talk before. He knows all the reactions to it, and how long he must pause to let those reactions play themselves out. "My dear sirs"—it pleases him to flatter the scum—"I suggest nothing criminal. Nothing violent, God help us all. Even the nastiest doxy may be missed—by her pimp, perhaps. No, what I suggest . . . it may be that you have a reliable paramour who would like to enact the role of Weeping Woman?

"A Weeping Woman is a very good way of procuring a cheap corpse. Suppose I am desirous of an infant, or a strong youth in his prime. Your Weeping Woman will beat on the workhouse door, crying, 'I am looking for my sister's babby, he but nine months old, left with a neighbour and now she says he is dead.' Or, 'James, James, my brother James, he was impressed for a sailor and now some say he is dead, these seven years I have not seen him' . . . so, you know, if the overseer suspects in the least and presses her for a description, she can say, 'But a shrimp-like lad of thirteen when he went to sea, how shall I know him now he is a man grown?' And as you will understand, it is not in the interests of workhouse officers to ask too many questions, because if she claims him for burial, the parish is spared the expense. I would recommend this to you as an excellent way, moreover, to obtain the corpse of a woman who is with child—an object of great interest to me. Only rehearse them in this way: 'My sister, my dear sister Kate, if I had known her shame I would have taken her in, why should she drown herself so?' It is advisable to practice with your Weeping Woman beforehand, taking the part of the overseer, so as to prepare her for any unexpected turn that the interview may take. But as you will understand, the life of a Weeping Woman is limited." He pauses. "Because she gets known, you see. Because she gets known.

"You may say, it is an easy matter to discover when the rich have expired, you may find it in the gazettes. But ask yourself, am I man enough for a mausoleum? Can I rip marble apart? The corpses of the rich are often guarded, and their coffins of lead; even if wooden, they bury deep, and their coffins are of such sturdiness that sometimes the lid may need to be sawn across, which is not the quickest business; and you must beware spring traps and trip wires. Reflect then, that the corpse of the plutocrat, his wife, or daughter has no inherent superiority to that of the beggar and his moll. All corpses are welcome to me, unless putrid or poxy.

"A paupers' grave, as you know, may contain several corpses within one deep pit, and is therefore likely to yield well per hour of effort—but do not be tempted to descend into pits, however well-charged, for I have known men to collapse, overcome with poisonous emanations. What you cannot do with hooks and ropes, do not do at all. Keep your feet on level ground. Do not jump on coffins, for rotten coffins will not take your weight.

"Keep a keen watch on the hospitals, so that you know what paupers are to be admitted in the next day or so, for what operations. Those of you who are porters in the hospitals have the advantage—look out for those persons dying with deformities and distortions, such as vastly swollen heads—those are of great interest to me also. Avoid those with noxious, offensive tumours, as they sting the students' fingers. Remember that Jews bury early; where a corpse is wanted that must be very fresh, their cemeteries are very likely, very likely indeed.

"Be advised that for the corpses of young children I pay by the inch. For the first foot, one shilling. Thereafter, ninepence per inch.

"Do not delay on account of clawing out the corpse's teeth. I am aware that persons will offer you a price for them, but I will give you the teeth, if I don't want them myself, and you are much better to extract them in the safety and good light of my own rooms than you are to salvage them by lantern's gleam in the clammy dark, with the dogs howling about you and the watch on its way.

"Certain artists will come to you, asking you to bring them material. Bear in mind that the character of artists is bad in general, and their pockets are not deep. You may find yourself turned away with any number of excuses: 'Ah, I had in mind a larger man, I had in mind a younger woman'—and there is the corpse on your hands, rotting, and all your labour lost. Do not trust artists. As for me, you will find me a ready purchaser. Hard but fair.

"Remember, speed is of the essence. I will say to you what I say to my students. Do not trifle with corpses, or perform indignities on them, such as flipping the male's penis, or introducing instruments into the orifices of young women. Be sure, be rapid, take a pride in your work. Do nothing to increase the disgust in which you are already held.

"Do not steal the grave clothes. *Do not be greedy.* The theft of the body is in itself no crime, for whereas an animal's carcase is property the carcase of a man is not. But if you take away the shroud or the winding sheet, you commit a theft. In any case, the value of such articles, at second-hand, is not great. Throw them back, on what remains of the coffin. Then fill in, leave no loose soil, smooth all.

"Leave the grave as you found it. No slovenly workmanship—for that conduces to suspicion, and suspicion conduces to lying in wait, and lying in wait conduces to apprehension, and apprehension conduces to a mob, and a mob conduces to a smashed pate and a broken leg, and a noose if you are unlucky. Therefore, should you find any little object laid on a grave—such as a flower, a shell, or an arrangement of stones—study how it is placed, carefully pluck it off, save it, and then replace it once your work is done.

"You will want a table with the phases of the moon. This I will provide."

"You said that before, sir," a man ventures.

"Aye." He takes out his handkerchief and wipes his sweating face. "I said it before."

six

Alone in his work room, John Hunter broods. Around him are the tools of his trade, his blades and saws, and his hand steals towards them, as if he cannot help himself. Why think? Why not experiment? And see where experiment leads? Don't conjecture. Don't waste time on it. Observe.

Swiss peasants told Mr. Linnaeus that the worm *Gordius,* if it be cut into a number of pieces, each piece can yet twitch; and if the pieces be put into water, each will grow the head and tail it lacks. Men of learning had scoffed at this as superstition, when they could have found it to be true, if only they had *experimented* and spent a little of their time cutting up worms. In our day, it is not the Oxford man, or the scientific dandy, who is the hero of observation, it is the peasant, the Hunter, the man with his snout in the soil—he who does not say, "This is contrary to nature," because he allows himself to be endlessly astonished by nature's variety and perversity. He has no prejudices, no expectations. He bears no ill-will to any life-form. He has often cut up worms, for when you live in a place like Long Calderwood you learn to make your own entertainment.

Besides these habits of mind, what skill does an experimenter need? He needs patience, deftness, and the ability to think of doing what other people would deem completely pointless.

Take M. Trembley. He was admittedly a gentleman, or at least tutor to a gentleman; but he had a humble cast of mind. M. Trembley crept about in ditches, dredging up vegetation and thick brown slime. With delight, and through his magnifying glass, he observed the hydra, a freshwater polyp with arms shaped like horns.

M. Trembley kept his retrieved polyps in glass jars. He cut them up with a small pair of scissors, lengthways, crossways, every-which-ways. There was no killing them. He minced them and he grafted them, he made three of one. He watched them regenerate. Some grew eight heads. One day he sneaked up on a polyp with a hog's bristle and turned it inside out, forcing its posterior through its mouth. M. Trembley was awarded a medal. For a while, polyps were the top fashion. Even great ladies were seen pursuing them, draggling in ditches. Then the fashion changed, and the virtuosi moved on to electrical experiments.

What lessons do we pluck from M. Trembley's work—a model of its type? Disbelieve everybody, even Aristotle. Write down your methods. Experiment. Do it over and over. Cut finer. Distrust general rules. Cut finer still.

They'd been thinking about a triumphal procession, but the trouble is, Joe Vance said, you can't have a triumph without horses, and your ordinary horse set beside your giant looks like a low dog, a spaniel. So you've got to hire Percherons, and they don't come cheap.

"They have to be caparisoned with cloth of gold," the Giant said.

"Yes, the caparisons, that's another expense," Joe said. "What do you say we just walk around? It's only a short step."

So they set out on foot along Piccadilly. Crowds in the street gaped and jostled and craned their necks. Joe shouted satirically, "Look your fill, cheapskates, pop your eyes," and produced a box, which he rattled in front of them.

They came to Spring Gardens. "Nice high ceilings, I thought," Joe said. "Claffey, don't spit on the floor, if you want to spit go out in the street."

"Out in the street, is it?" Claffey glared.

"Now, now," Joe said. "No cross words on our first day in our new house."

Their exhibition room, above the cane shop, was airy and lofty. Their own quarters, at the back, were meaner, and yet ostentatious. "Bedding is ordered up from the landlord," Vance said. "He has a woman sees to it, but we must provide our own linen. I know a supplier, as it happens . . ."

"Fine linen," the Giant stipulated.

"Fine, to be sure."

"A pair of sheets you can draw—swish—through a woman's bangle."

"If you will," said Vance.

Jankin said, "Have we to sleep up in the air on platforms?"

"They are called beds, Jankin," said the Giant. "You have come across them in stories."

"Will I not roll off, when I am dreaming, and injure myself?"

"Very likely," said the Giant.

Jankin pulled at his sleeve. "Mester, have you ever, you know, slept in a bed?"

"No," the Giant said. "I never have, Jankin. There's no point, really, when your legs from the knees have to dangle elsewhere, and if you turn in the night you crack your knuckles on the floor. Better stay level, ground level."

"Still," Jankin said, "it's a great thing to be a giant. I wish I were one."

"But as you're not, you can relish the thought of an easy night."

They heard a door bang, and a female step, and an exclamation. "Gentlemen all!"

"But we know you, Miss," Pybus said.

It was the girl from the cellar, with the shining face and the silver hair. "I am employed here by your landlord, since he has forgotten how to speak our language, just to see that the night-soil man hauls your shit away, and that you are not setting fire to his premises, or painting on the walls. I hope you will not do that."

Joe Vance grinned. "You'll take a drink?"

"I will not. I work for the landlord, he gives me a meal a day and a penny for straw."

"Straw? Straw be damned. You can share with us," Joe offered.

"Or I can cut my throat," the girl said calmly. "Either will do, I suppose?"

Joe scowled. "That red-head, the one with the kerchief. From the cellar. What's her name?"

"Bitch."

"What?"

"That is what we are all named, here in England. Shift my shit, bitch. Scrub my floor, bitch. Lift your skirt, bitch, shut your eyes, soon you'll come by a nasty surprise."

"This isn't right," the Giant said.

"Not pleasant, but highly reasonable," the girl said. "Suppose one of ours is taken up and questioned: What is the name of the woman who cut that man, what is the name of the woman who took his purse? Bitch, he says. Yes, I know, says the magistrate, but what is her name? Then our boy rolls his eyes and says, Bitch: or at least she has no other name I ever heard."

"I see it," Claffey said. "I understand. It's a grand scheme. But from day to day can we not . . . ?"

"You can call me Mary," the girl said.

The Giant said, "That's all-purpose, too."

That was a happy week. They had a sea-coal fire, and a handy pump nearby. Bitch Mary found them a hedgehog, to keep down beetles. She also showed them what they could eat: oysters and Yarmouth herring, and hot gingerbread from a stall, fat pork and dumplings from the cookshop, bread and cheese. The vegetables tasted of smoke and the milk tasted of water, but they never minded. Joe Vance was in high spirits. He bought Bitch Mary a blue ribbon, which she put away for Sunday. To drink, they had gin and beer.

I have ordered a white bear from Greenland.

Opportunities for the dissection of whales too seldom occur; I wish I could get a whale. I wish I could get a tame lion, not very old, or the foal of a camel sent to me in a tub of spirits.

Jankin came in, wailing from the street. What's the matter? they asked him.

"A woman asked me if I wanted to buy a song. I said yes, and she took my penny and she gave me this." Jankin held out a piece of paper, which he had screwed up in his fist. "I said, 'That's not a song, miss,' and she got in a lather, and she said, 'Bog off, bog-head,' and everybody laughed."

"He ought not be let out alone," Bitch Mary said.

Joe Vance took the sheet and straightened it out. " 'The Debtor's Lament,' " he said in disgust. "'Tis forty years old to my knowledge. You've been had, piss-wit. Next time you want a song, sing it yourself."

"What age are you, Charlie?" Joe Vance said.

The Giant stared. "What age? I'd never considered."

"I need it for the press. We are going to have an insertion in the newspaper. To draw the notice of the best class of person to the fine spectacle you present."

"Let's say one-and-twenty. It's nobody's business, is it?"

"One-and-twenty it is. The Tallest Man in the World, at home at Spring Gardens for a limited period only, having recently returned from continental triumphs, exhibiting in Cologne, Paris, Strasbourg, and Amsterdam, where Mr. Byrne has been received by the finest and most genteel society and made a conquest of the ladies' hearts."

"But that's a lie!" Claffey said.

"It is usual to lie in advertisements, Claffey. Allow me to know my trade."

I would like to get a nest, an old cuckoo, and a young cuckoo.

"And then you'll be meeting the press," Joe Vance said. He looked around, at their quarters. "It's a bit bare, do y'know? We could do with fancifying it a bit."

"All costs money," Claffey said.

Said Joe, "I'll lash out a bit. In anticipation of large returns."

By this time, John Hunter is a great man, with his house at Jermyn Street and another out in the country at Earl's Court. It is there he keeps his collection of specimens, now growing huge, and his caged animals, who roar and paw and bellow through the night. He has first refusal of all the beasts who die in the menagerie at the Tower of London, and amongst animal sellers deals with Mr. Gough, with Mr. Bailey of Piccadilly, whose trade is chiefly in birds, who will get you anything from a linnet to an eagle, and who is so obliging as to extend credit: with Mr. Brookes, who had crossed a dog with a wolf, and who gave him one of the puppies. (She was a nervous bitch, who habitually ran out into the road and would not come back when she was called. She was given to trembling and starts of terror, which caused some citizens to mistake her for a mad dog and murder her.)

As for Earl's Court, who knows what comes in and what goes out—everything from leopards to gnats in a jar. There are the bees, silently industrious in their many hives, the seagull to be fed for a year on barley, the vat of live eels sent every month from the fishmonger, and the single swallow tamed by Mr. Granger, condemned forever to get its food dead instead of live and on the wing, and never again to see the African coast. As for the opossums, he must have had a dozen over the years, but breed? They *cannot* or they *will not.* Perhaps they propagate by a method as yet unknown?

On their second day in their new home Pybus brought an orange and a lemon, and they all examined them. They cut up the orange and sucked its juice, smacking their lips, and then they cut up the lemon and attempted the same. Bitch Mary exploded in laughter at them, holding it back until she saw their puckered faces and stinging lips.

"Laughing like a country girl," Claffey said fondly.

Mary ate everything they ate, and was already fuller in the face. Her hair was paler than the lemon's flesh.

Oxford Street was the problem: Claffey and Pybus and Jankin gawping its length, wanting things. Even by night, when the whale-oil lamps shone, they would promenade, their toes turned out, imagining themselves with a two-shilling tart on one arm, and in the other hand a cane with an ivory knob. The Giant was kept close until his prepared debut, but Joe was out and about, making his excuses for an hour off here and there and coming back with a smirk and his pocket lighter.

"Course, we'll have to borrow a little bit," he said. "It's the usual thing. I'm an agent and I know about it."

So it came to the day when they were making a wish-list:

A tea-caddy and a spoon.
A tilting tea-table, mahogany: very convenient for restricted space: space being usually restricted, when giant on premises.
A teapot and the correct bowls for tea.
A toothbrush and some toothpowder in a jar.
A salt cellar.
Some glass candlesticks, which are all the go.
A clock.
A trumpet.
Two siskins in a gilt cage.
A warming pan.
A mousetrap.
A writing set.
Some sheets of wallpaper with views on them: with an Indian

prince riding on a pony, and a slave holding a parasol over his head. And hunting dogs. And cranes. And flowers.

"Gentlemen of the press," said Joe. He held his arms up, as if he were brandishing flaming torches. The gentlemen sat on chairs that Joe had hired, ferreting in their wigs and picking their noses. The Giant was behind a green curtain, crouching. "But lately from our continental triumphs," Joe said. He looked about the room, smiling, side to side; trying to stimulate a round of applause.

"Yerg-h-h," said one of the pressmen, yawning in his face.

That set them off all over the room, "Yerg-h-h," in a broken chorus.

Behind the curtain, the Giant cleared his throat. His intention was only to warn Joe to cut it short; there was a crushing pain in his thighs and calves, and his kneecaps were fighting out through the skin. But the sound produced a sudden sharpening, a sobering, in the room. "By God's balls!" one man exclaimed; all sat up straighter.

Joe was taken aback. He looked down, and saw the Giant's toe peeping from under the screening. "Without further delay," he announced, in the voice of a hero, while simultaneously scooping at the curtain. It stuck—the rail being Claffey's carpentry—and Joe found himself dragging on it, wrapped in it, fighting a bout with it, until the Giant simply unhooked it from its moorings and stepped forth into plain view.

There was a moment's silence; then a low whistle of admiration ran around the room. As it subsided, a ragged clapping began, and was taken up by one pressman after another; each uttered his own obscenity as he clapped, and each stared, and one said, "Dammit, he has snapped the curtain rail," and the Giant looked down at his own hand and saw that oh yes, so he had.

He smiled. It was an uncalculated, accidental effect, but they had taken it like bait. Joe Vance was pink with pleasure; error had turned to triumph. "Please, Mr. Byrne!" He gestured towards the capacious wooden chair, a throne in type, that Pybus and Claffey had been working on for three days. Its construction was rough, naturally, but they had been out shopping and got a length of red plush, which Bitch Mary had draped in a most artistic fashion across the seat and arms—careless, but classical.

The Giant leaned down and tested the chair seat with his hand. Testing was his necessary habit with all chairs, stools, benches, and stone walls. He lowered himself, crossed his legs suavely, and saw and heard the pressmen gasp in amazement. "What a tableau he makes," Joe whispered to Claffey. "What a tableau indeed!"

For what had they expected, the press corps? They'd looked for some rumblethump, some tattery freak with his head on backwards and a cyclops eye. Instead they've an aristocrat of height. Said Joe Vance loudly, for the benefit of the scribes, "There's enough lace on his cuff to deck every altar in the Vatican."

There was a pause, a hiatus. The Giant looked around the room, half-smiling. After a moment passed, he raised one eyebrow. Ah, St. Silan, he thought. St. Silan could cause death just by raising an eyebrow; suicides used to wait up, hoping to catch him at dawn in a quizzical mood.

One pressman, nodding nervously, quivered to his feet: "Sir Giant, how do you account for your parentage?"

By a piece of business pre-arranged with Joe, the Giant drew out a length of muslin, three feet or so, from his sleeve, and dabbed the corners of his mouth genteelly. Only then did he begin to speak.

"I was conceived on the slopes of a green hill, known as a sacred place by the men and women of my nation. My mother was a green girl entirely, and my father came out of Scotland, possessed of a raw and tartan heart."

It was not the answer he had practiced with Joe. Joe's was tedious, tortuous, something to do with Noah and his Ark: who went in and came out, and a large number of stowaways, undetected by the great man and his tribe of relatives.

"Sir Giant," said a second man, "are there any more at home like you?"

"Alas, my upbringing was solitary. There were some few paltry fellows—two in particular, the brothers Knife, conceived on top of a haystack in our parish—who had a conceit they were tall, and who used to extort money from the credulous; but I know nothing of their lineage, and look upon them rather as sports of nature than as what I am myself, a descendent of the ancient native lords. And there is a lad named Patrick, Patrick O'Brien, who has sometimes claimed kinship with me—who has indeed, I hear, sometimes claimed to *be* me—but he is no more high, sir, than you are a Chinaman."

"So accept no substitutes," Joe said brightly. "Charles Byrne, Tallest Man in the World."

Claffey said to Pybus, under his breath, "I wondered when they'd mention Pat O'Brien."

A languid fellow rose, at the back of the room. He *ah-hemmed* before he spoke, and fluttered his hand to draw attention to himself. "You have lately been at Cologne, your publicist states. Tell me, what wonders did you see there?"

"Oh, Smartarse," Joe breathed. "There's always one."

"Why, they have a little church," the Giant said equably. "They call it a Dom. I'd take up residence in that fair stadt, only to avoid a boff on the head every time I want to say a prayer. The place wants finishing, mind, but the three kings have a golden house there." He leaned back on his throne. "Among the French églises there are some pretty little chapels, one they call Notre Dame in Paris I remember. Amsterdam is most picturesque, with rivulets running between the houses."

"All right?" Joe called out to the gentleman. "Happy, are you?"

The Giant reached over to calm him, but with the tip of his middle finger he accidentally caught Joe under the chin. There was laughter, scattered applause.

"Picture his snuff box," one fellow said. "It would be like a soup-plate."

"Picture his linen bill! It will be like the national debt."

"Picture his . . ." And the speaker choked; the whole room fell back as one, and opened its eyes wide, and fanned itself with a hand.

Just this morning Joe had said, "Play it up a bit, about the ladies, Charlie. Will you do that? Will you do that for me?" He had been every inch the impresario, purring and preening, but his guts turning over with nerves inside; now he stood grinning, caressing his bruised chin, neverminding about it, his gratified lips open and his greedy pink tongue just peeping out between.

The Giant leaned forward, causing the front row to sway back. "As you suspect, gents," he said, "my organ is proportionate."

A new sound filled the room: wistful, sibilant, yearning. The Giant sat back while it played itself out, melted sighing into the corners of the room. A young fellow spoke up, gathering his courage: "Yet women say, the women I know . . . they say size don't count."

"Do they?" The Giant held up his hand, scrutinised his fingernails. "And they say that to you, do they? Ah well. One can imagine why they would."

A little laughter, edgy. "I see, gentlemen," the Giant said, "that you wish me to enlarge. On the theme. On the subject. It is proportionate, as I say. Will I stand up again, so you can appraise my proportions? No; there is no need, I perceive; you can view my assets while I recline. A Tower of Ivory," he explained, "at the base of which they fall, stunned. Not but what they do not recover themselves; the fainting, I think, is out of politeness largely. And then, gentlemen, their rhapsodical sighs and moans—but I see by your faces that you already know those sounds, albeit only in your imaginations. First they try to scale this tower—the ambition is natural to them—with their slick little tongues like the tongues of kittens. When I am satisfied in that way, I put out my little finger and flip two or three of them on their backs. When I say 'two or three,' when I say 'them,' I speak advisedly—for I have about me every night an eager set of the female sex. They fear . . . they fear indeed—but oh, it is their fear that delights them! And gentlemen, when dawn comes, I am the complete gallant. Which of you can say as much? I have a fellow in Covent's Garden who brings each morning a selection of fresh bouquets, wound up with ribbon such as ladies like. Each morning he fetches half-a-dozen, at five o'clock—and when, three or four times in the week, more are needed, I have a smart lad who goes to run and tell him. And when you, at some stale hour, are rolling from your mattresses, and roaring for your piss-pots, and grinding the yellow pills from your eyes—and when, I say, your foetid molls are trolling forth, booted from your couches, unwashed, fishy, chafed between the thighs, slowly dripping your lukewarm seed—my douce delights are receiving their bouquets, with pearls of pretty laughter. Each one carries within her a giant baby. How can she not conceive? My seed is propelled within her like a whirlwind. I do not spill forth, like little men—I come like the wrath of God. When the years have flown, and my dear delights are grandmas, they will need only to think of the business we transacted, and their dried parts will spin like windmills in a gale."

Clarke has got a preparation of an extra-uterine pregnancy. The foetus lodged in the tube and began to grow there, the mother dying of it. It is a very fine preparation, and I mean to have it. I have said to Clarke, will you give it to me? No, I will not. Surely you will. Positively, I will not. You will sell it me then. No no and no. Then if I see you in a dark alley I will murder you, I said. Clarke half-believes me, for he sees the flush rise up in my cheeks. I half-believe myself. I must have it.

“That’s my boy,” Joe said, when the pressmen had surged out, chattering, into the street. “It’s the very way to treat them, a touch of the flattery and a touch of the imperial contempt.”

Yet there was something nervous about Joe: he was glad and sorry, he was thinking it had gone well and yet it had gone too well, it was out of his grasp a bit. As the gentlemen had exited, he had called out in his brightest voice, “Eleven till three, five till eight, six days a week, only half-a-crown a person!”

One of the gentlemen had stopped. “Look here, sniveller, don’t be crying your wares as if your giant were a hot pie—get a handbill printed.”

“A handbill?” Vance gawped. His hand closed on the man’s arm. “Where would I get that?”

Claffey dug Pybus in the ribs, and turned down his mouth.

“Why, go to a jobbin’ printer,” the pressman drawled. “And will y’ quit molesting my cuff?”

Joe took his hand away as if the sleeve were heated iron. He was desperate not to offend.

“Jobbin’ printers,” Claffey said to him afterwards. “That’s what I heard mentioned by a few. I suppose you know what they are?”

“Them?” Joe guffawed. “Isn’t my uncle the chief jobbin’ of the parish? Leave it up to me.” He turned on the Giant, rubbing his buttocks, complaining. “I came down with a rueful crash there. There was no need to turn me arse-over-pate to make a comedy.”

“I was trying to calm you,” the Giant explained. “My finger went astray.”

Later, Jankin stole up and said, “Giant, have you ever, you know . . . with a lady?”

The Giant was impressed to know that Jankin had not believed a word he had said to the newspaper men. He confessed, "I am a perfect stranger to the rites of Venus."

"Ah, then it's only me," Jankin said, melancholy. "The virgin of the world. If Joe would put a twopence in my pocket, I could make my addresses to a lady."

"Has he given you naught?" The Giant fished a coin out. "Buy a sweetmeat. Offer it to a lady, do you understand? Don't take out your diddler and ask her to suck it."

"Can I not have a bite of the sweetmeat myself?"

"If she offers. But give it her nice, wrapped up. Not with your fingers stamped in it."

"I wouldn't know how to address an Englishwoman. Could I address Bitch Mary?"

"Mary? Leave that alone. Claffey would yoick your entrails out."

The Giant stooped, and passed his hand over the seat of his throne. "Here." He pulled out a great iron nail and held it up. "Is this your work, Jankin? All the time I'm boasting about Paris and Amsterdam, and this little device boring into my buttocks."

"Sorry," Jankin said.

"Ah well," said the Giant, and snapped the nail in two between his fingers.

"It's an experiment," Hunter said. "You have heard of an experiment, have you?"

"Is it a disease?" the pauper said.

"Y're way off, man," said John Hunter. "An experiment isn't a disease! It's the thing that imparts the knowledge that makes a man of science like me able to cure the disease."

"Is that an experiment?" the pauper said. "That blade you've got out your drawer?"

"We call this a lancet, not a blade. Brace up, can't you! My man Howison gave you full information that you were to be in an experiment, you came here to my house on that understanding, and if you don't like it you can walk out that door."

"And if I do, will I get a penny for my trouble?"

"No, not a farthing, but my boot up your backside. Trouble? You? What trouble did it give you, to step along to a gentleman's house and be treated civil? What were you doing else? Watching a cockroach race, were you? Oh, I'd be very sorry to drag you from a cockroach race, I'm sure."

Calm down, John Hunter. Get a grip. Those arteries of yours are hardening, that blood pressure is shooting up the scale on the instruments not yet within your ken. You feel the blood in your ears, ker-clunk—and if you were to glance into the plain pine-framed oval of mirror that lights the north wall of your consulting room, you would see your cheeks, with their outgrowth of ginger bristle, dappled with a flush as rosy as a girl's. What is modesty in her, is choler in you: not healthy, John.

When I look out of the window and see the cats after my pheasants and digging up my flowers, I scramble for my gun, but by the time I get to it the cats have run away. This makes a spasm in my chest.

The pauper cowered against the wall, his hands covering his privy parts. "What are you going to do with me?"

"Give you a wee prick," Hunter said.

"Will it hurt me?"

"Naw, man." He plucked at the pauper's shielding arms.

"Will it make my parts drop off?"

"Naw. It'll do you good. In fact, it's a dose of medicine for you, with my compliments."

The man stared. He had never heard of getting something for nothing.

"Look, now," Hunter said. "Let me show you how it will be." Patiently, he unbuttoned himself, and took out his tackle, easing his balls through the placket. Scarlet against its bush of orange hair, his cock was as vivid as the part of some obscene tropical monkey. It lay glowing in the palm of his hand, looking as if it might break out into some violence.

"Come on now," Hunter said to the pauper. "Fair's fair. Now show me yours." The pauper's eyes were riveted. "I never saw one on a Scotchman before," he said. "Are they all that colour?"

"Gaze your fill," Hunter said pleasantly; it was an effort to be pleasant, but it would gain him his end.

"So what . . . so what are you going to do?"

"I will demonstrate," Hunter said. He reached behind him and picked up the lancet from the table. "Now watch." He rolled back his foreskin, bringing the instrument a whisker from his flesh—indicating with it. "I will just give you a tiny touch, right there. A man of vigour, such as yourself, you'll not feel it. Then you may button up, and I will give you sixpence."

"Eightpence," the pauper said.

Hunter breathed freely. "Eightpence," he said.

The pauper straightened himself a little from the wall, but his shoulders were still hunched protectively as he began to undo his buttons. He had no underwear whatsoever, and smelled rank. Hunter reached forward and seized his pale, shrivelled organ. The pauper yelped. "Get off me!"

"Calm yourself, man. I must examine you, to see are you healthy."

"Am I?" The pauper's voice shook.

Hunter pushed back the foreskin with his thumb, as if he were shucking peel.

"Looks all right to me."

Absorbed, he hardly noticed that his own organs were swinging freely, until a sharp draught from the window caught him. Would have been more professional to button up, he thought, more workmanlike—if Wullie could see him now—but what the hell. He took a firm grip on the pauper. "Hold still now." He pulled forward the man's foreskin, jabbed it. In a split second, he slicked it back, then jabbed the head of the organ.

The pauper gave a yelp of horrified surprise. "All done," John Hunter said. But not—not all done—not—good grief, what was this? The pauper was snarling like a diseased dog, drool running from his mouth and his eyes blank. "Take a hold of yourself," Hunter shouted. "You act like you've taken a mortal wound."

The man's wrist shot out. His hand was splayed to a claw. It was starved, but it was sinewy. He grasped Hunter's wrist, his right wrist. His other hand closed over the knuckle. He drove Hunter's arm down, down and in, slamming it towards his body. The lancet, trapped in the great man's fingers, drove hard into the flesh, and ripped a trail of blood from his organ—blood shockingly brighter than the sanguine flesh it sprang from.

With a whoop, the pauper relaxed his grip. The lancet fell to the floor.

Hunter stared down at himself. He moved slowly, reaching for a cloth and dabbing.

The pauper, who seemed to have grown a foot taller, was buttoning himself up with an almost jaunty air. "Now I'll have my eightpence," he said.

Ah well, Hunter said to himself. Perhaps it is a happy accident, after all. I should have needed to keep the man under observation, and he did not seem a very reliable pauper; perhaps he would have run away or got transported or hanged, and I should have lost the chance of observing his symptoms as they arise. And without a doubt, every time I asked him to appear before me he would have wanted money. Well, here I am, and within two or three weeks I will have the pox myself, and what could be more convenient? I can make my observations and recordings from the comfort of my own armchair. And I won't send myself a bill either.

seven

The experiment had taken place on a Friday. Saturday, nothing. Sunday, a teasing itch. The itch gone by Tuesday. But then the hard chancre: a cause of rejoicing. His theories soon to be proved, on his own flesh.

He holds his pen as if it were a surgical tool. He begins to record, knowing what he can now expect: the attack upon the glans and urethra, the discharge of many colours, the bleeding, the irritation and swelling of the testicles, the muscle spasm which causes the urine to be voided by jerks; suppuration, fistula in perineo, pains in thighs, vomiting, abdominal pain, and colic. His handwriting is small—to save paper costs—but always legible. After the valerian, musk, camphor, cold bath, hot bath, electricity, and opium it will be the mercury cure. But not for three years yet. A man must have time to make his observations. Physician, heal thyself; this saying also applies to surgeons.

Meanwhile, experimentation continues. He becomes interested in the venereal blotches that break out on the skin. He inoculates a pocky pauper with matter from another person's chancre, and is interested to find that chancres form. To be sure it is not a fluke, he does the experiment again and again. He inoculates another pauper with matter from an ulcerous tonsil—with no result—and with a gonorrhoeal discharge: this latter produces a chancre. Theories whizz around and around in his head. He takes out his organ and stares at it. The mysteries of the universe are here.

A woman of twenty-five comes into St. Georges' Hospital with florid skin symptoms, and he detains her till he has found a person with buboes who has not been treated by mercury, and in whom he can be pretty sure that the buboes are venereal and not scrofulous. He injects matter from the buboes into the skin of the woman of twenty-five, and for good measure injects her with fluid from her own ulcers. He writes up his case notes.

He has become used now to the thick, snuffling voices of those who are affected in the throat. Unfortunately for them, their lesions don't scab over, as the act of swallowing keeps the parts always moist. Deafness is frequent, with suppuration of the ear. Effects on the whole constitution are to be anticipated; a couple of years on, the deep ache inside begins, the pain that seems to bloom out of the bones. Nights, it's worse. He lies awake thinking of experiments he might make. The question of the drowned persons haunts him. They used to roll them over a barrel, or hang them up by their heels, thinking the water would drain out. He turns over and over in his bed—his solitary bed. The spaniels yap, the mastiff growls, the leopards roar beneath the moon.

He is satisfied the venereal plague cannot be spread by saliva. He has tried his best and failed. It is not, then, like the bite of a mad dog. Some say it stays in the blood, year upon year. He cannot see this. How it can be. There are those who have too much imagination, its findings unbuttressed by results.

That summer the Giant grew rich. He washed in Castile soap, and made the purchase of some decanters. His followers ate green peas and strawberries. Joe Vance played with the writing set, and Pybus, Claffey, and Jankin haunted the skittle alleys, the cock-fighting, the prize-fighting, the dog-fighting, and the bull-baiting. "If we go on so," said Claffey, grinning, "we will have tamboured waistcoats like the quality, and silver buckles to our shoes."

"What do you mean, if we go on so? I am not likely to shrink."

"You're of a testy temper these days," Joe observed, glancing up from his calligraphy.

The Giant, by evening, was often tired from exhibiting, and they woke him with their drunken stumbles on the stair. Gin and water was their only tipple now, and they brought it back for Bitch Mary.

When the patron's half-crown was given over—the price of viewing the Giant—Joe Vance would give back a tin token; this was the system favoured by all the best shows and spectacles. Select groups of ten or a dozen a time were admitted, and they came in a steady stream all through June and July: through those months when the streets steamed and the poisoned water trickled from the pumps and London shit baked in the ditches, when milk turned and fish stank and the blinded birds in their prisons of gilt were stunned and silent in the heat. Sometimes, a smaller party would be admitted: ladies, rustling, faces glowing, frou-frou of petticoats and scent of musk and powder and cut flowers dying. Often they asked to converse with the Giant—this he did very easy, very civil—and they not only paid their half-crown but left a handsome tip on top of it. He dreamed of their tiny feet on London staircases, skittering like the feet of mice.

"I don't think he should have his percentage on the tip," Claffey said, nodding towards Joe Vance. "After all, it's not earnings, it's a token of esteem, more a sort of prize or reward to Charlie for being tall."

"So Charlie should have it in his own pocket," said Pybus.

Joe's eyebrows shot up. "You want your nose punched out of the back of your head?" he offered. "You want me to press on your cheeks so your eyes zing out of your skull and go bouncing about the room?"

August: sunlight slipped like rancid butter down the walls. Joe returned to the book he was reading, frowning and gnawing his lip. It was a book about a prince, and Jankin was waiting for him to finish and tell stories out of it. "He that writ the book is called McEvilly," Jankin said. "Joe Vance's grandad knew his grandad."

The Giant looked up, smiling. "That's right, Jankin. Weren't they both turf boys together to the O'Donaghues of Glen Flesk?"

The horizon was bright, these evenings, with the pearl-like shiver of noctilucent clouds. But dark at last fell; blood-red Antares blazed over the city.

"For all the prodigies of nature, there's an awful lot of blawflum," said Hunter to Howison, his trusted operative. "Do you remember Mary Toft?"

"She that gave birth to fifteen rabbits?"

"She that did not."

"And yet the court itself, sir—did not the prince of Wales send his surgeon down to Godalming?"

"What? There was a procession of them, man, rode down to Surrey to view the tomfoolery. And did the fools not fetch her up to town, and lodge her handsome? The woman had a vast distended belly, to be sure, and plenty of activity inside it, but that hardly diagnoses rabbits." Hunter snorted: for sometimes people do snort. “It’s fairy tales, that’s what it is—fairy tales, and rabbit skins and scraps smuggled under the skirts and groaning and moaning from the lass while the coins are chinking into a basin. Sir Richard Manningham had the right of it, he threatened her with an operation to relieve her condition—aye, he showed her the knife.” John Hunter chuckled: for people do chuckle. “I tell you, her belly soon deflated. No, Howison, I wouldn’t give you threepence for a woman pregnant with rabbits. I wouldn’t cross the street to see it—no more would I ride out over wild heathland where I might have my purse taken.”

“Ah, sir, you might have your purse taken any fine night in Bond Street.”

“Not that ought is in it,” Hunter said, sighing, and scratching himself a little. “I am the greatest surgeon in Europe, Howison, it is acknowledged, and I frequently find myself as poor as when I was a raggedy scamp with a snivel nose and a hole in my breeks.”

It is a pity he has not got a hole in his breeks now, Howison thought, it would be convenient for him to ease his itch. “You have laid out so much in experimentation, sir,” he said, “and in the purchase of specimens.”

“And on Mrs. Hunter! Do you have any idea, Howison, what that woman costs me per annum *in sheet music alone?*”

“I have no claim on gentility,” said Howison. “The women I know will open their legs for oysters and gin.”

“Stick to your own kind, that’s my advice. If I had not the damned expense of her minims and her crotchets, not to mention her nightcaps—she must have lace, Howison, on her nightcaps—I would be able to purchase a savage.”

“I could get you a black, easy. Dead or alive or anywhere in between.”

Hunter wrinkled his nose. “Your London blacks have lost their virtue. They are bronchitic and gone slack. No, I want a free savage, the dust of the bush still upon him, his wanton yodel rattling through the clear pipes of his chest, his tribal scars still raw, his cheeks and ribs fresh scored, his parts swinging and unfettered . . ." Unlike mine, he thought, breaking off in a sulk, for it had become necessary for him to resort to a suspensory bandage.

Howison did not like to be worsted by circumstance. Hunter employed him for his resource as well as his brute strength and steady hand. He knew his master was mean as well as skint, but he knew also that he could find ways of laying his hands on funds if the right subject for experimentation came along. As if reading his thought, Hunter said, "I cannot just purchase from a seaman—for then my savage will have been spoiled, its sweating body swaddled in a tail-coat and its guts churning with weevil-biscuits and porridge. Oh, I know what you will say—go out to savage realms, and choose for yourself. But then, I am advanced in years, and the pepper of my temper as a Scotchman makes me unsuited to a voyage in the torrid zones of this world."

Howison hoped that John Hunter was not hinting that he should go in person, off to Patagonia or Guinea, in search of some cicatrised wailer with webbed feet and his head under his arm. He, Howison, had got his feet under the table at the Dog and Duck in St. George's Fields, and had hopes of confluence with the landlady's god-daughter at the Swan with Two Necks: at least, she was supposed to be her god-daughter, and he had never heard of her charging anybody, not so far. Howison, for luck, turned his money over in his pocket; it was the night of the new moon.

Jankin had come home at dusk, inhumanly excited: "We have been to see Dr. Katterfelter's magic show. He appeared a black kitten in a man's pocket, he did, Charlie, so he did!"

Joe didn't bother to look up from his book. "Katterfelter is a common conjuror."

Claffey and Pybus came in, shouting, "Here, Bitch Mary!"

The girl came, from the corner where she rested from her

labours; in this corner she settled herself on rags, like a dog's wife scraping a nest for whelps.

"You see this water?" Claffey said. "You see this water in this bottle? It is no ordinary water. This water has been blessed by His Holiness the Pope and specifically magnetised under license by Monsieur Mesmer, the sage of Vienna and Paris. Its name is called Olympic Dew. The queen of France bathes in it every day."

"Ah well," Bitch Mary said. "Not enough for a bath, more a little facial splash—but I thank you, gentlemen."

"But look here," Claffey said. His fierce freckles were glowing; his peel-nailed finger went dart, stab at the bottle's label. "See just here the cross, that means His Holiness, and here's the painted eye within a triangle that means Monsieur Mesmer has blessed it himself with the animal spirits—"

"You sure he didn't piss it?" Joe inquired.

"Or the pope piss it?" said Mary.

"For shame," Jankin said. "His Holiness does certainly never piss."

"His water is drawn off by angels," the Giant said, "without pain or embarrassment, of course. What would you say that we all stay in tonight and I tell you a story?"

He hardly dared to raise his head.

Jankin said, "The dwarves with duck-feet, is it?"

"I hope if you met them, Jankin, you would not be so impolite as to mention their duck-feet."

"Small chance of that," Claffey said. "You claim that they occur in Switzerland. We could not prove you wrong."

"And I could not prove me right," the Giant said. "But at the mere breath of scepticism, I fall silent. What interest have I, Claffey, what possible interest could I have, in convincing you of the existence of web-footed Alpines of diminutive habit?"

Claffey gaped at him. He could not understand the question. His face flushed up to the hair-roots. He felt his big moment with Bitch Mary had been spoiled.

"Besides," the Giant said. "You know I do not like dwarf tales. They are too sad. I do not like them."

At nine-thirty that evening it was still light, but it had begun to drizzle. Bitch Mary, crouching by the window, made a squeak of surprise; they all swarmed—except the Giant—to see what it was, and within seconds Claffey, Pybus, and Jankin were down the stairs and out.

"What was it?" said the Giant. He felt disinclined to move; his legs ached.

"It was an Englishman," Bitch Mary said. "Walking beneath a canopy on a stick."

"Umbrella," Joe said, bored. "The apprentices are always turning out against them. It's a fact that they are easy prey because carried by their clergymen and the more fussy and nervous type of old fellow."

"Such as," Bitch Mary said, "those who think rain will run through their skins and thin their blood."

"The boys like to throw stones after, then chase the fellows and collapse the tent on their heads, making them sopping."

"Ah well," said the Giant. He yawned. "I'm sure they wish they had such a lively time in Dublin."

That night the three followers came back battered and bruised. Pybus, in particular, was shockingly mangled. They were cheerful and brimming with gin, and had hardly stepped over the threshold when Claffey demanded, "Give us Prince Hackball, the beggar chief!"

"Hackball?" the Giant said. "I remember when you yearned for stories of the deeds of kings."

Joe had brought him a flask of spirits, the necessary sort. His head was clear and ringing, his speech precise and tending to echo in his own ears: as hero's speech should do.

"Hackball," the lads chanted. "We want Hackball."

"Hackball was prince of beggars," Claffey said. "Two dogs drew his cart."

"For God's sake." Joe looked up in irritation from his prince book. "I think you confuse him with Billy Bowl, a man with no legs, who went along through the city in a wood basin with an iron skiddy under it, and his arms propelled him forwards. One day there were two women provoking him and calling him deformity, and did he not flail the flea-bitten she-cats? For which he was brought up—Charlie, was he not, support me here—"

"For which he was brought up before the justices, and—his bowl and skiddy being damaged in the fracas—he was brought to court in a wheelbarrow, and sentenced to hard labour for life."

The Giant put his head in his hands. The bones there seemed to pulse, as if bones were living, as if they were fighting. The skin at his temples seemed frail, and he wondered if inner provocation would break it. Pybus and Claffey went away to bathe their contusions. The Giant was afraid that, under the new moon, his followers had got a taste for riot, and he wondered what they would do when the nights were lighter and the moon was full.

At full moon they went out with cutlasses, spits, bottles, and pokers, for an informal fight with some Englishmen. Afterwards they chased a Jew, finding themselves part of a light-night mob with drink taken, and passed on from Jew-baiting to window-breaking to tearing up railings.

The Giant was alone in their chambers. It was a hot night, and he opened the casement. The hour was ten and it was still and grey. The cries and groans of Londoners, their bedside prayers, drifted to him faintly on a breeze dank as the Honduras. Behind him the candle flame guttered, threatened to fail: as if underground. By its feeble light, he stretched out his hands and examined them. I need, I do so need, he thought, a stick for measuring. It may be that I'm seeing what I want to see—or, to be exact, what

I don't want to see. He stretched out his hand, to test its span. His new shoes were tighter, but then a man's feet swell in the summer heat, it's what's to be expected. He crossed the room and ducked experimentally under the door frame. This was more informative. He had been in these rooms some weeks now, and the instructions for ducking were coded into his knee-joints. And it was not his imagination—in the last fortnight, he had to bend them deeper.

So.

He drifted back to the window. He looked down into the courtyard. Bitch Mary was standing by the gate, talking to a woman. He saw the pale glowing curve of the child's skull; her hair streamed silver. She reached up her arms to embrace the woman, and as the woman stepped forward the Giant saw that he knew her; she was the red-head from the cellar, who wore a green kerchief and had punctured Joe Vance with her wit. He almost called down to them; but no, he thought, I will be poor company. He felt in his bones and his gut the truth of what anecdote and observation had taught him: a giant who begins to grow again does not live long.

Hunter stalks alone, by the crepuscular Thames. He thinks, I have had no opportunity of making actual experiments on drowned persons. Not his fault if he hadn't. Still, it's not the season for suicide. Spring kills the melancholy rich man, who seeks relief from his humour; in late autumn the beggars drown themselves, for better reasons, after they have spent the first night of the season in a trough or hole awash with icy rain. Women bearing disgraceful children drown themselves at any season of the year. If his people were only vigilant, he would have a constant supply of them, either for reanimation or dissection. Do not assume she is dead. Beat the water out of her. Tenderise the trollop as if she were a piece of meat. Squeeze her spongy lungs as if you had them in your very fists. And when they drown themselves in the depths of winter, when the ice is breaking up, then there is every hope—for the cold, he already suspects, brings on a shock to the system, which holds a specimen in a kind of suspended life. Properly treated, such a person may be revivified, though he has been under water for ten minutes, twenty minutes . . . where is the frontier of death?

What if, he thinks, this state of cold might be artificially induced, and suddenly induced—if a man in possession of his health and spirits, let's say, were to volunteer to be packed around with Greenland ice . . . the cold would numb him, the cold would sleep him, and if the supply of ice were constantly replenished. . . . *I want to get a white bear from Greenland* . . . might he not sleep away a year or so? Or would his organs fail? It might be a welcome specific for bored men-about-town: an elegant excuse for failing to visit maiden aunts and plain heiresses. "I am iced up till next June, alas . . ." Or a good way to evade your debtors, of whom he has plenty. Imagine Howison, ushering them into his freezing-cabinet: "Gentlemen, you may see John Hunter now—but John Hunter is unable to see you." Yet he doesn't think, not seriously, of icing himself. His man Howison is a reliable man and wouldn't let him thaw, but all the same, he has work to do, the progress of his disease to observe.

The clamminess of his skin, the natural clamminess of the humid night, has turned to a cold sweat that drips down his back. He thinks of the dead. His mind turns to them often. Corpses are my library, he would say, when an importunate bookseller pressed on him the vast *Death Encyclopedia* (illustrated) of Dr. Knogus-Boggus of Amsterdam or Professor Schniffle-Bum of the Vienna School of Medicine. Experiment, he would say, see for yourself, go in with the knife and lay bare and see what you see.

And yet the dead defy him. Something in their nature. The principle of life has gone out of them—the principle that he knows exists, but he is not sure what it is. He tells his men, you can never be sure, with the hanged no more than the drowned—reanimation is possible—do not pick their pockets, for fear of future prosecution. But when the body is brought to him, and stretched on the slab, it is frequently the case that he finds tears in his eyes. He says to himself, come now, John Hunter, this is mere dissection room nostalgia, mourning for the days when you used to cut shoulder-to-shoulder with Wullie, before you had your schism over the nature of the placenta; it is nostalgia for the early days, when you were a raw boy and not all Europe's veneration.

But in his heart he knows it is more than that. It is the dead themselves who move him to tears. Numb to the scents of a hot summer's evening; deaf to laughter, blind to clouds. Not just still, and not just cold, but waxen, quenched, extinct—and gone . . . gone where? This is what anguishes him: the question where. He wants to haul them back, with iron hooks. He wants to question them: where? He wants to know if there is a soul and if the soul can split from the body and if so, what is its mechanism for getting out—a usual orifice or permeation through the skin? What is the weight of the soul? If you pushed him, he'd guess a couple of ounces, not more.

A surgeon does not present himself often at a sick bed, and he is not able to make the moment-by-moment observations available to the physician: the changes in colour and respiration that signal that the wolf death is creeping up the stairs. The surgeon's patients die violently under his hands, or he judges them beyond his aid and he disdains to practice on them, for there's no point in mutilation without hope of cure. One would relieve the pain of any human creature, but what is the point in attempting to part a woman from her rotted breast unless she is hale and fit and likely to live to say thank you and pay her bill? Come: let's be practical.

But the dead are not practical. They are no use except for cutting up. They answer no questions that are put to them. They lie and stiffen, in their perfect self-containment. They defy understanding. Hunter's mind dwells on that split second when everything that is, is lost beyond recall. When life and hope go separate ways.

❧

Pybus and Claffey burst in, disturbing the Giant in his first dew-like sleep. "Wake up Charlie—we have been to a tumult."

"Not again."

"It was a rare tumult—we rioted against anatomies. It's one who cuts up persons after they're dead and pulls out their hearts and eats them."

"Their hearts alone?"

"They like to follow after the carts when it's hanging day, and they pay over money so they may get the body and then the men—"

"And then the men—"

"—and then the men get all in a big mob and try to knock down the hangman—"

"—steal him away, the dead body—"

"—rub his neck till he's back to life—"

"—rub neck and chest."

"Or give him a decent burial."

"But still if they can't get enough hanged, they go into the graveyards, these anatomies, and dig them."

"Eat their liver and boil their guts for tripe."

"Yes, yes," the Giant said. "So you rioted a little while, and then you—"

"There was a man in a carriage, and we took out his horses, cheering, and we ourselves went between the shafts and pulled him, with some Englishmen."

"Who was this man?"

"We don't know his name. He was the government. One of the horses that was unyoked was led away by a man from Limerick, Fancy Boy Craddock he called himself."

"He was not the government, that we pulled along. He was against the government. That was the government, when we broke their windows."

"Oh, was it."

"Sometimes, when the anatomy is just going to make the first cut, the corpse sits up and seizes him by the throat. Sometimes the blackguard dies of it, he drops down with shock."

"Does this happen often?" the Giant asked.

"Oh, two or three times in the year."

"You wouldn't think he'd be quite so shocked, then."

John Hunter is at home now, and hears a great knocking at his back door, and hollers, "Howison, man, shift yerself."

Two men, heaving with effort, dumping their burden on the flags, cursing quietly, fetching out a knife, and hacking at the rope; one sack off, hauled over the head, and he sees a livid, blotched face—

Swarming up beyond Howison, whose mouth is already opening to argue, Hunter thunders, "I have seen this corpse before."

"True," says the salesman, fawning. "All respect to your eye, Mr. John Hunter, you have seen this corpse before. But I've brought it back at a nicer price."

It is left to Howison to boot the fellow out of the premises, the fellow and his confederate and his rapidly depreciating asset.

John Hunter sighs. He wants company, Howison discerns. Weary and wary both, he steps up the stairs. Hunter is brooding amongst his books—of which he has a few, though he says corpses are my library. "Here," he says, "did I ever show you this curiosity? Never mind the text, man, feel the binding. It's the skin of William Thorburn, that slew Kitty Flinch, the Wrexham Belle. It cost no little trouble in the flaying of him."

He sees Howison's face, and a mild contempt there. "Do you

not believe me?" The pitch of his voice has shot up; his pulse rate risen; heat at his temples.

"That the flaying was difficult? Oh yes, it would be a job for an operator with a delicate touch. I mean just that I have heard other gentlemen say they have the same book on their shelves, so you must wonder of what extent was Thorburn, to furnish so many libraries?"

"So I am cheated, am I?" Master yourself, John, he says to himself. Easy, John. "Ah well, it is a trifle. It is no matter." He slides the volume back in, beside the *Osteographia* of Cheselden. "Do you know of the Enfield child?" he says, casually.

Howison pricks up his ears. "Eighteen inches round the thigh, at the age of nine months and two weeks."

"Over three feet—they allege—at the age of a year. A most famous prodigy. Pity he died."

"Passed away at eighteen months." Out of respect for the deceased, Howison removes his hat and holds it to his chest.

"And gone where? Who has the skeleton, that's what I'd like to know."

"There is"—Howison clears his throat—"there is a giant exhibiting in Spring Gardens above the cane shop. If your reverence would like to see him . . ."

"What does he charge?"

"Half-a-crown."

John Hunter snorts. "Negotiate a lower rate, or free for me. What's the use of eminence, if you've to put your hand in your pocket for every freak that tawdles through the town?"

"I'll try," said Howison, yawning.

"Away to your bed," Hunter tells him. "And leave me to my thoughts."

Alone then, he opens the shutter and lets the night into the room. They are at Earl's Court, and he hears the bark of his bears, his watchdogs' snarls. He seats himself, and pours a glass. Late at night, the mind refights its old campaigns. There is no such thing as gunpowder poisoning. Get me a savage. Or a dwarf. Or a giant. Half a crown! For a giant! Still: what cannot be cured must be enjoyed. Pay out, see the fellow. Might be of interest. Might be.

Remember the night the Eskimos came to dinner? George Cartwright brought them, the trader: knowing Hunter liked curiosities. They were a party of five—two men, two squaws, one infant. Cartwright had lodged them at Little Castle Street, showed them about the town, and presented them at court. Considering that they were savages and ate raw flesh, they were able to sit up to the table quite decent. After dinner there was a misunderstanding; he thought to show them his collection, but at the sight of the bones hanging up they became frightened into dumbness. He found out, afterwards, that they thought they were the remains of his previous meals.

All these Eskimos took the small pox, and died at Plymouth, except for one squaw. He had missed the chance to get an Eskimo for his collection; you cannot handle a small pox corpse, the risk is too great. Still, they are engraved upon his physiognomist's memory: their heads were long and large, their eyelids folded, their skin bronze. He had little opportunity of hearing their voices. The younger squaw smiled pleasantly, though not after she had seen the skeletons.

He heard later that the hair of the dead woman had been cut off and carried back to Labrador and given to her friends, and that this was the means of introducing the malady into those parts, over three hundred dying of it at once. He does not know if this is true.

He remembers how on the night the Eskimos left his house, silent crowds stood in the streets to watch them go. Lamplight shone on their flat brown faces, and he thought they wore expressions of distaste.

John Hunter presses his head in his hands. Before he fell out with Wullie, they might have been here together at the end of the day,

Wullie saying, Damned coarse stuff this, call it claret, I wouldn't stir it into the meal to fatten a hog . . . always querying and carping, his queue neatly ribboned, a quizzical finger laid to his cheek, his abuse as crude as any Scottish boy. But now I am here alone, and true darkness coming down.

He takes down his favourite book, *De Sedibus Causis Morborum.* On the Sites and Causes of Disease. He opens it on his knees, and stares down at it, sightless. His mind moves slowly. Giovanni Battista Morgagni, the distinguished author, performed over seven hundred autopsies personally, and usually John finds the volume supplies endless diversion. But tonight he cannot be amused. He frets, he turns a page, he stands and shelves the book. Nothing will do but skull arrangement.

Candle in hand, he descends to his work room.

Under the moon the copper vat gleams, the copper vat for boiling flesh from bone. The eyeless stare at him; the nameless specimens grin and peer, a scribble of light on the curve of their jars; the lungs long-dissected take in one whistling breath. In his day he has been heroic in experimentation. He has transplanted a human tooth into a cock's comb, and seen it take root. He has fed a pig on madder, so its teeth came out red-and-white striped. He has dissected a gibbon! He turns sharply; thinks he sees something in the shadows. The creeping of a polydactyl hand across marble . . . or perhaps the ripple of flesh and fluid, as conjoined twins elbow for space in their bottle.

He raises his candle. There are the skulls, in no particular order; or rather, in a chosen disorder, artfully hodge-podged so that no one can eavesdrop on his thoughts. He possesses the skull of a European man, an Australian aborigine, a young chimpanzee, a macaque monkey, a crocodile, and a dog. His stubby hand caresses the cold apertures, the tallow-coloured curves. He arranges them. Cróc. Dog. Macaque. A monkey is half-beast, half-man, he thinks. His hand, sweating a little, imparts heat and moisture to the bone. Chimp. Savage. European Male. John Hunter stands back from them. He sees patterns he has no permission to see.

And sighing, disarranges again; and back upstairs, his tread slow. Something is baying from the cages: something far from home. The moon strikes down on Long Calderwood, strikes a cold kindling in the thatch, stirs brother James in his long-time grave; the night breeze sighs through East Kilbride, and rifles the tops of trees with the fingers of a Chick Lane pickpocket.

"Grave news," said Joe Vance, coming in with a paper in his hand. "It's concerning Patrick O'Brien."

"Oh yes?" The Giant looked up, without much interest.

"They say he's grown a good ten inches since we left home."

"But Paddy is only a boy."

"Yes, and the more time to grow! The way he's going, Charlie, I can't see how he won't top you in the next three months. I can't see how he can avoid being less than eight feet and a half. And the worst of it is, he's threatening to come over."

"Well, let him," the Giant said. "Maybe after his novelty has worn off we can go two-for-the-price-of-one. Besides, it will be company for me. Giants, you know, have much to say when they meet each other."

Joe stared at him hard. "I don't think you quite have a grip on this, Charlie. I know Paddy's agent, and he's a slick bugger. All Paddy has to do is set himself up, advertising as, let's say, 'P. Byrne, Tallest Man in World,' take a room somewhere central, and steal away a good half of your future customers. Some jobbin' will be paid to run off a few handbills, and there'll be you traduced and trampled, Charles. Then even if we come at him with the full force of the law, he can easy go to Bath, or where-so-ever, get the easy pickings, and deny you the fruits of a lucrative provincial tour."

"Oh. Am I going on tour?"

"It was in my mind."

"Call it a progress, there's a good man. *Tour* has a low sound about it."

"Don't say that word *low*. I dream by night that I see Patrick as tall as the treetops."

The Giant leaned forward, and opened his hand. He clapped it across Joe's chest, spanning it. "Send out Pybus for a tool of measurement."

"What can you mean?"

"Look, Joe Vance. Come here to the table. Do you see this knot in the wood? Now, do you see there, what you might call a mark or score?"

Joe nodded.

"You see the space? A month ago, my fingers could not bridge it."

Joe stared at him. "You're growing, Charlie?" A sly grin crept over his face. "You're growing?"

"My head is lengthening and stretching. I feel the pain deep in my bones, as if the close knitting of my skull were beginning to ease itself, beneath my scalp, and unstitch. I feel a pain in my jaw, as if the swing of it were to be tested, as if the swivel cannot support the greater weight that is to come. My feet are bursting from my boots, Joe. See here—I've had to slit them. My knee-joints and ankle-bones are oppressed."

"Oh, good, good!" said Joe Vance. "By the private parts of Mary, this will give him a check, Mr. so-called Patrick Byrne!" His honest blue eyes were blazing. "Let's have a drink on it," he said.

In September, the days innocent of chill, they went to Bartholomew Fair. The Giant was confined indoors, as usual, but they told him everything when they got home. Dancing dogs and monkeys. Musical operas, a French puppet show with Mr. Punch and the Devil behind doors.

"We had some cabbage to eat at Pye Corner," Pybus said, "and a slice of beef each. Joe treated us."

"That was handsome of him," the Giant said.

"We ought to go down, Charlie," said Claffey. "Get you a booth."

"What, like a dancing monkey?"

"It's where the crowds are, and where the crowds are, that's where the money is."

Pybus blurted out, "Joe Vance says you are growing."

"Do you not see the change in me?"

"We see you every day," Claffey said. "If it's gradual, we might miss it."

"But it's proved by the measuring stick," Pybus said. The late sunlight caught his red hair and made a fire in it. "By God, Charlie, I'm glad I decided to come on this voyage. Our fame is assured. We shall ride in sedan chairs!"

"Carry one, more like. That's an attribute of Irishmen." He looked up, at Claffey. "So—you have your own notions of taking me to market, do you? You think you know better than my accredited agent?"

Claffey puffed himself up. "I certainly know this town, Charlie, I can say I know this town. What say we ship Joe back to Ireland to fight it out with Paddy's people, and I take on managing you, at a reduced percentage?"

The Giant studied Claffey. Narrow grey eyes close-set. An unintelligent expression, but an avaricious one. "So," he said, "did you bring anything for Mary, from your day at the fair?"

"Oh, he did," shouted Jankin. "Oh, he did and I liked the Devil behind doors. Oh, he did bring her Cyprian Wash-Balls."

"Come forward, Bitch Mary," shouted the Giant.

Mary crept from her bedding. She stood before Claffey without meeting his eyes.

"Claffey means to pay you his proper addresses," Pybus said. "He is advanced in the art of courtship. He don't mean to force you against a wall, but wait till you're ready and you give him the word."

"That'll be enough," Claffey snarled, practically spitting in his ire. He took a shuddering breath—calming himself, so as not to split and rupture Pybus on the spot: only because, afterwards, the woman would have to clean the floor. "Mary," he said, "I am giving you these Cyprian Wash-Balls, but on one condition."

"And what is that?"

"I have seen you at the gate these nights, when I am coming in, talking with that whore that wears a green kerchief."

"Bride is her name."

"I want you to keep away. Never greet her more."

"Because she piqued your vanity," the Giant said. "She did so, that night in the cellar. She worsted you and Joe both."

"Not for that," Claffey said. "But because she is a whoremonger. The very tips of her fingers are creeping with disease."

"I'll do what I must, and when I must," Bitch Mary said. "Till then, I reserve my opinion. Will that content you?"

"I don't like it," Claffey said. "But go on—there you are."

"What is the use of these Cyprian Wash-Balls?"

"To keep your hands white."

Bitch Mary stared down at her paws. "I don't know," she said. "I'll have to think. I like your addresses, Claffey, but then you may decide to quit these shores, which I know I never shall."

"Ah," said Jankin, "you are easier with their language than us. Even Charlie has not your sweet manipulation of the tongue."

Claffey felled him with a blow. "What do you know of her tongue? You stuff-brain, you couldn't turn your tongue around a corner!"

Mary ran for the bucket and a cloth. A large part of Jankin's brains looked to be burst on the black floorboards of their room. Indifferent, she swabbed Jankin and the planks. She hummed softly as she worked. Pybus stood over her, drooling, looking down at her laboring flanks. "Bride says she can offer me lucrative opportunities," Bitch Mary said.

Night's drawing in. By candlelight again—just one for economy—John Hunter is compiling (speculatively) the index to his great work on venereal disease.

Decay of the Testicle	*45*
Carbuncles or Excrescences	*48*
Odematous Inflammation	*75*
Of Sarsaparilla	*112*

And the Giant, turning in his sleep, hears Francis Claffey coming in, and singing on the stair.

There's not a mile in Ireland's isle,
Where the dirty varmint musters,
Where'er he puts his dear forefeet,
He murders them in clusters;
The toads went hop, the frogs went pop
Slap haste into the water.

Claffey: the entrepreneur.

And a pause, some bumping and boring in the dark. Then the Giant hears a different voice, though still Claffey's; it is broken, distant, sober. "Give me to drink I beg you . . . a bottle of mountain dew."

eight

"Howison, go out and fetch me some paupers. I want to make them vomit."

Howison only stares.

"Vomiting, man, vomiting. I am doing an experiment on it."

"Yes, your reverence. But what shall I say is the going rate?"

"Oh, God dammit, man! It's not as if they'll take permanent harm. Would they do it for a penny?"

"I doubt it, sir. If you're going to make a man throw up, you must at least give him the price of a meal. Threepence, I'd say. Though a woman would do it for less, and you can always find an Irishman who'll undercut the rate for a job."

"Females and Irishmen let it be, then." He goes

away grunting, wondering to himself if Irishwomen would be cheaper still.

He has a theory that it is the action of the diaphragm that produces vomiting, not, as some jimmy idiots maintain, the action of the stomach. It is the diaphragm, that puissant muscle, contracting itself and dipping into the cavity of the abdomen . . . but how to prove it? You would have to feed a subject an emetic, then paralyse the diaphragm. He cannot imagine what physiological mayhem would ensue during the experiment, if his theory is correct.

Moving day. They are leaving Spring Gardens for new rooms on Piccadilly, at the sign of the Hampshire Hod. Joe is hovering between two possibilities: either load everything onto the Giant and walk him round, or hire a carrier. The first course is cheaper in the short term, but has the long-term disadvantage that the Giant will be shown off free.

"We might as well auction this swivelling mahogany tea-table," Joe said. "'Tisn't as if we could afford to treat ourselves to tea."

"How can't afford?" the Giant said.

"It may have escaped your imperial notice, but since the dog days our trade has declined."

"We are victim to fresh sensations," Bitch Mary said. "Come to town for the fall."

"Charlie could keep us in tea," said Pybus. "He has a ton of money, I have seen it. Or at least, I've seen the great bag that it's in."

"Yes," said the Giant. "Joe, I must broach again this question of a strongbox."

From the earliest days, Joe had encouraged the Giant to keep his money with him at all times, saying, "Who would dare rob a giant?" The Giant had said, "Should we not have an iron-girt strongbox?" Vance: "The strongest box is vulnerable to the ingenious London thieves. If you were at home and on guard, there would be no need for the device, and if you walked abroad, you could not carry it with you. It would be a social inconvenience. It would look gauche. No, better keep your cash on your person."

Now, Joe Vance, who was no more a fortune-teller than you or me, had dimly foreseen a day when he might be the happier for this arrangement, without being able to imagine precisely why. Since the Giant had hardly been allowed out to spend anything, he had now accumulated an amount that Claffey and Pybus could only guess at, a sum that was secret between Joe and his account book. Their fingers and eyes might have been tempted to stray; but O'Brien slept with his savings for a pillow, while Vance kept his ledger under locks.

The day of the move, Bitch Mary sat crying in her corner. "Come with us," said Pybus. "Ah, do, dear Bitch."

"I cannot. I have promised to work for the landlord for a penny a day."

"Joe Vance will give you a penny a day, and more."

"But I have contracted my work, until I have paid off a debt."

"What debt?"

The girl's brow wrinkled. "I hardly know. Bride knows."

"Whose debt is it? That bawd herself?"

"Bride was a mother to me," Mary said, "when I came off the boat. True woman of Ireland, she plucked me from the quayside and certain ruin, for I was being enticed to go away with a vendor of maidenheads. Bride took me to a shelter and gave me bread and a blanket, and she and the blind man, who is called Ferris, brought me to London together. I lodged then at Henrietta Street, until I came to this place, one penny per day, clean straw and my food all found. As for the debt, I don't know whose it is, but I know I am bound to it, and if I go with you to the sign of the Hampshire Hod the landlord will come after me and fetch me back and knock my teeth out, for so he always promised if I strayed away."

"Who is the landlord?" Pybus said.

"His name's Kane, he's a Derry man."

Pybus was shocked. "One of our own?"

"Of course. Or why would your agent Joe Vance be doing business with him?"

Pybus thought, this is a poor state of affairs. He waited till Claffey came in. Claffey had a white moustache and beard, from drinking milk from a bucket he had seen standing in the yard. Pybus didn't like to mention it, but it was hard to concentrate on the conversation. "Mary won't come," he said, "she's got a debt, she don't know how great."

"A debt?" Claffey said. "That's not good news. She's young for a debt." He snivelled hard—the morning was dank and rheumy—and Pybus saw the milk-vapour rise towards a nostril, as if it might ascend upwards to his brain. It was not hard to imagine Claffey an infant. Fists clenched, beating the breast. His hair sparse—as now—his heels drumming while he sucked a rag.

Pybus blinked. His attention had been elsewhere. Claffey was saying, ". . . leave it then. I thought her a tender little morsel, though she has hardly any titties, but if she comes with a debt I shall be wrapping my bundle and on the road elsewhere."

Pybus went to the Giant. "Bitch Mary has a debt," he said. "She is forced to slave."

"Let it be paid, let it be paid," said the Giant. But then he flopped back, his great head subsiding onto his store of money. More and more he wanted to sleep these days, and less and less did he fight the impulse. His strong snores drove Pybus from the door.

Pybus said to Vance, "Bitch Mary has a debt."

"So she does" was the genial response. "And must work to pay it."

"But for how many years?" Pybus said.

Joe shrugged. "Who knows how many? And should she sicken and die, another will pay it in her place." He stood up and stretched. "Time to shift ourselves," he said. "Come on, boy, why are you standing with your mouth ajar? Hurry up and box our effects, the carrier will be here in a half-hour."

For Joe had opted for medium-term profit, choosing not to parade the Giant through the streets with a close-stool on his shoulder and their bird cage and siskins dangling from one finger. "Rouse up, Charlie," Vance shouted from the doorway; this failing, he crouched down on the floor, and bellowed in the Giant's ear.

The Giant turned over, muttering, and his arm flailed, and his blanket lifted like a galleon's sail filled with stormy air. Whoosh! He sat up. Startled awake. "Would you consider, Joe, that you pay me the proper respect?"

"Due to what?"

"Due to a prodigy and a scholar."

"Shite and shite again!" said Joe. "Your school was in the hedge, and when the English cut it down you had to confess your learning complete. Your scholarship consists of a few Latin tags and your native talent for talking that which I above mentioned."

The Giant yawned. Joe was tapping his timepiece. "Get up off that floor. From noon today this patch of floor reverts to the Derry man, and he has already let it to a merman and his school."

"What Derry man?" asked the Giant. He rubbed his eyes, tentatively. They felt as if they were bulging out of his skull. "What merman? What school?"

An hour later, they were at the door and ready to go. Joe said, "Look, considering that we've gone to the expense of hiring a cart in order to keep you *sub rosa* and *in camera*—"

"Who's the tag-man now?" The Giant smirked.

"—can't you stoop double? And we'll wrap your head in a sack?"

"Wrap your head in a brick, Joe." The Giant took a swig from the chased silver flask he kept always in his pocket. He waited till the warmth hit him, just beneath his clammy and floating breastbone. At once he felt strengthened, from the inside out. He swigged again. Waited. Felt a resurgence there, a little stir of dead nerves. His feet, these days, were increasingly far away. His fists also. He swept up one fingertip, and bringing it through a vast arch placed it not unprecisely on Joe Vance's shoulder. "Come along, thou great classicist. Down to Piccadilly we go, tag, rag, and bobtail."

He thought, why should you wrap my head in a sack? When God has wrapped it in the clouds?

"Still," Claffey had said. His narrow eyes downcast, his red knuckles kneading.

"Still. Debt may not be so much. Maybe she cannot count."

"Don't think of it, Francis."

Joe Vance had never before used his familiar name. He felt flattered.

"Put it to yourself this way. The landlord has been paid a sum down, not for me to guess at what it might be. Call it a retainer, call it what you like. He contracts to feed her and give her an easy scrubbing job, keep her for a year or whenever she gets a bit of hair below and a bit of swelling up top. Then she can be traded out, and the investment gets paid."

Claffey rubbed his head. "Do that much more," Joe said, "and you'll cause another bald spot. I've never known London wear out a man's hair so fast."

"I thought," Claffey said, "that there was a prime trade in little skinless flesh—I mean, not heads, but little girls. So I was told by a man I met in Dover Street. I was told that there are gents who will pay five guineas to force a nine-year-old."

"You thought you could pass off Mary as nine?"

"She's very small and low."

"Oh yes, but Bride Caskey—"

"Is that what she calls herself?"

"Bride, who has the experience, says that she will not do as a nine-year-old or even a twelve-year-old, for those gentlemen want the appearance of innocence if not the reality, and she says Mary hasn't got it. She says she is tractable as all these girls are, but that she looks puzzled, when she should look frightened. That she will insist on talking, when she should be dumb."

"And so?"

"So Bride thinks it's best to fatten her a year, and wait. Till she gets to an age when her expression suits her better."

Pybus hung around at Spring Gardens. He wanted to give Mary a flower. When she came out the door, though, she was rushing with her flaxen head down like a ram's, and wearing a hat that belonged to somebody else. She stooped, dashed, she didn't see him. She had a soiled bedsheet draped round her shoulders, flapping in the heavy air, and she had in her hand something weighted and clanking and skin-like, that is to say, a purse. He barred her way. "Pybus!" she said.

"Is that the Giant's purse?"

"Did you not see O'Brien bear off his money?"

"True, I did."

"So?"

"So is this the Derry man's store?"

"This is my back-wages. Bride told me how much to take."

"Are you coming with us to Piccadilly then?"

"I'll be seeing you." She tore off down the street, her plait whipping over her shoulder like a rope made of light.

The Giant did not care for the rooms at the Hampshire Hod. They lodged close under the roof, and he sometimes had to bend double, his arms swaying, his knuckles on his boots. Claffey declared he looked like the grand-daddy of an ape that he had seen on a chain at Bartholomew. What manner of man was this ape, the Giant asked, interested, and Claffey replied he must be a near relation of yours, Charlie, for he grunts as you do in your sleep, and though he was wide awake nobody could credit a word he spoke.

When that first evening Mary did not arrive, they were forced to make up their own beds and fetch up water. "The Derry man will have her under lock and key," Joe Vance said. "We must get another scrubber."

Pybus thought of the meeting in the street. He kept quiet. Good luck to her, he thought. "She might visit us," said Jankin.

When Bitch Mary had not appeared in three days, Jankin began to fret. Joe tired of his whimpering, and gave him a back-hander. But he did agree that they could go out and walk the streets and call for her, and—stipulating only that they should wait until dusk—that the Giant should come with them. "For you can see over the buildings, Charlie," Jankin said. "You can see into the back courts and over walls, and look into the high-up windows."

So it was, in the hour after the lamps were lighted, that Londoners at their supper were surprised by the giant face of an Irishman appearing behind the foggy glass. Some cowered and some cursed, and some called for their watchdog to be let out. "Mary, Bitch Mary!" called Jankin, in his piping voice. Children ran after the Giant—barefoot, bow-legged, toothless children, wilder than any they had seen—and one of them threw a stone which struck Joe smartly on the shoulder. The band did not stop calling until they reached the fields to the west, where they sat down and rested on the rippling black grass. The cold crept into their bones, and the Giant winced as he flexed his fingers, and reached up to knead the back of his neck. They went home to bread and some maggoty cheese. Joe had ceased to order up suppers from the cookshop. "Face it," he said, "trade's not what it was. We cannot keep up our standard as aforesaid, unless O'Brien here puts his hand in his sack."

"But the money is for my own purposes," the Giant said. "It is not for laying out in mutton pies. That money is to go back to Ireland."

"For why?" Pybus asked. "It's not as if you've relatives living."

"It's for rebuilding Mulroney's tavern. This time in dressed stone, with columns. That don't fall down. With marble fireplaces, decorated with urns and wreaths. With lyre-backed chairs for furniture, and marquetry tables inlaid with the fruits of the season."

"He has started to believe his own stories," Claffey said.

"With looking glasses surmounted by gilded swans, and consoles supported by gilded ladies with wings and their upper torso bare. With clock cases trimmed with laurel leaves and the sun with a smiling face. With fire screens with Neapolitan vistas on them, and serpentine chests with secret drawers. And a frieze with the nine Muses dancing."

The next night, Vance stayed at home sulking. He declared he had better things to do than be stoned by street-life. "Like what?" Claffey asked him slyly. "Sit and count the Giant's money?"

Joe did not know whether the question expected the answer yes or the answer no.

He scowled at Claffey. "You get above your station, rag-arse."

"I'll be taking my sack with me," the Giant said. His tone was serene. "That way, there can be no doubt whether anything has gone out of it, and there need be no harsh opinions. Tonight we look east, my brave fellows. I swear we will see a glint of Mary before the sun rises."

For he looked to find her, this misty night, seated by the grey smudge of the river, her hair streaming like a comet, and the sky's last deep blue pooling in her eyes; to find her in the nasty sites of Old Street by calling her name, or to hear her laugh in Clerkenwell. Oh Mary, darling of our hearts, have you set your foot on Pickle-

Herring Stairs? Are you hawking tripe or picking rags, are you scouring ale-pots in Limehouse or sifting ash on the city's fringe?

He left Jankin sitting on a wall somewhere, complaining of his feet, and lost Claffey to a game of dice and Pybus to a game of skittles. He stopped in a room of greased beams and smoky tallow, where he ate hot water gruel with some bread crumbled in it and garnished with pepper; he asked for a pat of butter, and the landlady said, what do you think this is, Holland House? He saw some bandits eyeing up his money bag, and stood to his full height, at which they left the room, muttering.

Later they were waiting for him, in strength, but he casually placed an elbow in the eye socket of one, tripped another bloody-nose squash on the cobbles, and nudged a third into the wall head first. Then he picked up their leader—he was tired, and wanted an end of it—and tossed him into a midden.

It came on to rain. Ambling home down the Strand, towards midnight, he glanced into a back court, and under a dripping gable he saw a woman he recognised, but it was not Bitch Mary. He had seen her last in Ireland, stepping between the puddles, her child riding high in her belly. He could not be mistaken in those lakes that were her eyes, or the white arms which her rags exposed. So she left the grave after all, he thought, the grave of her hero son. I asked her to share my throne.

He would not shame her by speaking; she was selling herself, it was clear, to Englishmen. He took a coin from his bag, and, as he passed her, let it drop into the filth at her feet. "Here." Her voice rang out, hard and empty. "Fucking freak throws his lucre at me." He turned back. Noted her tone: whore bred in Hoxton. He saw that her face was not the same at all.

Back at the Hampshire Hod, he troubled the landlord for spirits, and climbed the stairs.

"Did you get her then?" Joe asked. He was hunched in the corner with his prince book and a candle.

The Giant didn't answer. "I want to move from here," he said. "Insufficiently commodious."

"Listen Charlie, I've been thinking."

"Have you so, Joe Vance? Is that the wailing and grunting that carries from here to Ludgate?"

"Sarcasm doesn't suit you," said Joe, looking up. "Broken pates is more your line. What say we pitch you in a prize-fight with that small giant who's showing at the Haymarket?"

"No." The Giant sat down. "It is a man on stilts, and besides, I don't feel well. I don't feel right in myself, and I want to move house."

"The porterage fees are mounting up. What with your whims and fancies."

"It wasn't my fancy to come here. Anyway . . . you'd been thinking, you said."

"Thinking about that volume of money you're toting around. Would you let me transmit it back home for you?"

"Back to where?"

"O'Connor's cabin would be safe enough. The man who comes raiding is only looking for his rightful cows; he wouldn't be so brutal as to loom in and steal from Connor's chest."

"It's my Mulroney's money, you understand?" The Giant brooded. "Thank you for your offer, Vance. But I think I'll keep it where I can see it, for now."

Every night they lay at Piccadilly, the Giant dreamed of the Edible House. The travellers who arrive at the house begin by eating it, but it ends by eating them.

On quarter day they moved to rooms in Cockspur Street. Their new landlord—not so new, because it was Kane—checked them in, and ran through the inventory with Joe.

"Lucky we've brought our own fire-irons," the Giant said. "That black and evil-looking set of tongs is the devil's own implement, and the poker inspires me with disgust."

"One pot for boiling," said the landlord.

"One pot for boiling," Joe said. "Do we pay extra for the hole in it?"

"One cup for keeping salt. One iron candlestick—"

"Dented," said Joe.

"Dented, but functional. One bolster, any objection to the bolster? Anything to say about it? Fine. Two chairs with straw seats, one painted chair with a dint in the back, one three-legged stool. And you'll please not say that it wobbles for that's just what a three-legged stool don't do. Three tin pint pots. One jar for vinegar. A pair of green woollen curtains with barely noticeable moth holes. And a deal table."

"It's a table fit for vagrants," Claffey said. "Jesus, Kane, there's not a single piece in this establishment that a pawnbroker would look at."

"That's the idea," said Kane.

It was Claffey who followed him to the door. "Have you any idea of the whereabouts of the girl Mary?"

"No, but if I had I'd peel the hide off her."

"Because our idiot, Jankin, he is off his fodder, and none of us is too happy till we know she's not drowned or lost. Would you know the whereabouts of Bride Caskey?"

"If I knew where Caskey was, I'd call the watch and see her marched to Newgate. When your girl Mary upped and left me, she helped herself to my purse with a guinea in it, and I'd swear Caskey put her up to it." His eyes narrowed. "Why do you want Mary, anyway?" He sniggered. "You want to put her on the streets and live on her while she's fresh meat. You're after making an income for yourself and swaggering out as you used to this summer. Are you feeling the pinch? Your giant's not what they call open-handed, is he?"

"He is saving up," Claffey said. "To restore the Court of Poetry."

Kane stared at him.

. . .

Indoors, Joe was trying to put a brave face on it. "It's not the standard we're accustomed to, but we can soon impart the individual touch. Wait till I get my set of satirical prints hung up, that will raise the tone."

"Somebody's nailed this window shut," Pybus said. "And look at these rags stuffed in the cracks. When the fire's going, the air in here will be so thick you'd need a knife to slice it."

"The prudent and economical man," Joe Vance said, "has no need of silk bedcurtains, and makes do with linsey woolsey. As for this set of spoons—why, a philosopher would not despise it." Joe looked around at them, smiling. "I'm off to the jobbin' now. Get some more bills printed. I'm bringing your price down, Charlie. You're coming down by a shilling. It's to stimulate demand and appeal to a new class of investors."

"Is there any news of Patrick O'Brien?" Claffey asked.

"Yes." Joe didn't cease to smile. "They say he's booked his passage, and an entourage with him."

Their cage was set upon the deal table; and the siskins began to sing.

One of their first visitors after the price had come down was a low, strong-looking man with not much top to his head, with sandy whiskers and a big jaw. He sat at the back when the viewers were ushered in, and folded his arms and never spoke, but he never took his eyes away either.

"Jesus," the Giant said. "He ought to pay double, for the amount he looked. His eyebeams would slice through your flesh."

At the point where the usual questions were over—How does it feel to be a giant? Did you always want to be a giant? Can anyone be a giant or are you born to it?—Joe had risen as usual, softly clearing his throat, his fingers making tactful little whisking movements towards the door. The sandy cove had stepped forward, and as the other clients took their leave he asked, "Are you quite well, my good fellow?"

His words were Scotch, and sharp. But close to, his glance did not seem perturbing; it wandered, and he squinted more than a little.

"Am I well?" the Giant had said. "Not precisely. My feet are enlarged, and I feel the springy gristle of my ankles and knees to be calcined. My hands are swole, and my arms drag out their sockets. There is a raddling in my kidneys, and my memory fails. I have taken a hatred to strong cheese, my head aches, and I stub my toes as I walk."

"I see," said the Scotchman. "Anything else?"

"I feel a gathering of the waters of the heart."

"Ah."

Just at that moment, Joe Vance, who had been ushering out the clients, came bursting back. "Charlie, I've been wanting to tell you—I'd the letter just before we exhibited—do you know Mester Goss of Dublin, Goss that trained the intelligent horse?"

"How so intelligent?" the Scotchman said. "A horse that did tricks, did it?"

"Tricks you may call them," Joe said, "but they induced in Goss prosperity and fame. Why, the equine could count! It was exhibited through Europe. Surely you've heard of it, sir, or where do you live? Well, the thing is, Charlie, I hear now that Goss is training up a sapient pig. And I've been wondering, when it's trained, to make him an offer for it. Couldn't we do grand business, don't you think, a giant and a learned pig on the one bill?"

The Giant asked, "What is the name of it?"

"Toby. All sapient pigs are called Toby."

"Is that so? It is one of the few facts I had not taken under cognizance."

"Well, gentlemen," said the Scot, "I would recommend you take expert advice before parting with your money, and if it comes to a contract, insert a clause allowing you to return the pig if you are not fully satisfied—within a reasonable time, say, a calendar month, which will give you the opportunity of a fair trial." (All this time, his eyes are boring into Charlie; the Giant feels his bones will split open and the marrow ooze out.) "That's my advice and freely given, for I've seen a number of these so-called educated bears and the like, and it's notable that they don't perform nearly so well when they are parted from their first keepers."

"Perhaps they grieve," suggested the Giant.

"No, it is a code. If they can count, or tell fortunes, it's because the keepers have taught them a code."

"It's clever in itself," said the Giant. "I could take to Toby, if he knew a code."

"I wonder," Vance said, "would you invest in it, Charlie? The money out your sack? Or some of it? If I were to write a billet to Goss?"

The Giant rubbed his chin. "Could I feel your pulse, sir?" asked the Scotchman.

"I don't know. Do we charge for it, Joe?"

"A donation would be gratefully received."

The customer put his hand in his pocket, and slapped down a farthing. His mouth turned down. He grappled the Giant's wrist in his. "Hm," he grunted. "Hm." He began counting. "Hm," he said again.

Released, the Giant stood up. The customer came to his waist. "Are you in the physicking line, then?"

"No, my trade is other. Bid you good day."

Joe Vance stood looking after him. "He was a queer little pepper-and-salt gentleman, was he not? He tried to put us off our pig. Does he train creatures himself? I wonder. And seeks to get our trade?"

O'Brien said, "Have you heard of the Red Caps, small gentlemen of Scotland? They are four feet high, they carry a staff, their nails are talons, and their teeth long and yellow. How do their caps get red? They dye them in human blood."

Pybus came up the stairs, bellowing, "Are you ready for your supper?"

Joe bawled down, "What is that supper?"

Yelled Pybus, "It is herring."

"It is always bloody herring these days," Claffey said.

John Hunter, back at Earl's Court, surveys the space he has available. I must expand, he thinks, get better premises, somewhere central, and set up a gallery, where I can exhibit. Leicester Square strikes him as convenient; those environs generally. It will add to his fame and maybe bring some money in. He rubs his eyes. He rubs his head. I am ruined, he tells himself, by lashing out on specimens. Experiments will bring me to bankruptcy; I'll go barefoot for knowledge. My wife will leave me. And my friends desert in droves. There, he thinks, just there shall Giant hang. I will move that armadillo three feet to the left, and the giant bones will sway, suspended on their wires, boiled and clean; for the man's a goner. The freak says it himself; the tides are gathering behind his ribs, the salt oedematous tides. His digits no longer obey him, his faculties flag; give it six months, and the pagan object will be mine.

"So," Joe Vance said, "despising your scepticism as I do, let me set out to you how such a pig works. You lay out letters around him, on cards, and ask him to spell a name and he goes to each letter and points with his trotter."

"It's superior entertainment," the Giant said. "For those that can read."

"Then you put down cards with numbers, and give it sums to

do. After that, you put down letters again, and ask it to read the thoughts of the people in the audience and spell them out. Or tell their fortunes, as the Scotchman hinted. Sometimes, if your pig's the prime article, you can blindfold it, and it will work just the same."

"But would you trust your fortune," the Giant asked, "if it were told by a pig?"

"Well, I do so think," said Pybus. "For a pig won't give you a favourable one, to get a tip."

"The boy reasons well," Joe said.

"And if a pig said, beware of a dray coming up fast on your left and mushing you against the wall, well, you'd beware."

"But not if a human said it?" the Giant asked.

"You see, Giant," Pybus explained, "the pig wouldn't have any interest whether it came true or not. But if a human told it you, and the dray came up and dunted in your ribs, you'd suspect that the said dray was driven by the fortune-teller's uncle. It's what they call a ploy. It's to get future money off you."

"Well, well," said the Giant. "You seem wise in the ways of the world, all of a sudden. Have you been looking into Joe's book about the prince?"

Pybus reddened. "I cannot read," he said. "And you know it, Charlie. Still less any book in a foreign tongue."

"You much neglect your advancement." The Giant sniffed. "Joe, how are you to persuade the ladies to our show? And the fine gentlemen? For a swine do smell."

"There you are under a mistake," Joe said hotly. "There is nothing in the breed, inherently, to make it smell, and you speak out of gross prejudice, O'Brien, at which I am surprised. Goss's pig almost certainly does not smell." He spoke with more loudness than conviction.

Claffey said, sniggering in the corner, "Joe Vance is related to a pig, that's why he stands up for his tribe."

"Come outside, skin-head," Vance proposed, "and I'll pound

your liver to a fine paste that I will use to stop up the chinks in the door frame."

"Gentlemen," the Giant said, "your complaints are grating in my ears and your incessant quarrels are scratching around in my brain like a rat in a hatbox. Would you not like the story of Bernard Owen O'Neill, whose uncle when on his way to fish for trout met a man without a head?"

And from his shelf, Hunter plucks out a book.

Wm Harvey: "Blood is the first engendered part . . . blood lives of itself . . . blood is the cause not only of life in general but also of longer or shorter life, of sleep and of watching, of genius, aptitude and strength." Give me a piece of luck, he prays. Get me this giant. For I have never had a piece of luck. Brother Wullie has had it all.

He lays down the book. Takes up tourniquet, his lancet. The instrument punctures the skin. Tender swollen vessels. Draw off a little ounce or five. Never miss it. As he bleeds his recalcitrant apes, to make them quiet; subdue the animal excitement as it rises inside. Like garnet lava, like molten jewels, it slides down the sides of the china basin. His lamp gutters. A draught lifts the papers on his desk, their fibres oppressed by the weight of his writing.

Pybus, going out to piss in the yard, found Bitch Mary crouching by the wall. When she lifted her head, he saw a dark patch around her mouth. "Get me a rag," she said.

He tried to raise her to her feet. "A rag to staunch," she said.

"Never mind," he said. "Come indoors."

"I need a rag to wipe the blood from between my legs. I do not want a man such as the Giant to see how his countrywomen are reduced."

Wm Harvey, having observed the pulsating heart of the chick in a fertilised egg, misunderstood what he had seen, and reported that the blood had its life, its own quivering beat. Its vitality lasted so long as it was not shed. Once it was shed, the living principle escaped. The blood separated then into its dead constituents, some serous, some fibrous; into parts that had no existence in living blood. Its nature was transformed by death: corrupted, he said, resolved.

Mary was shaking with cold. Her hair was cropped, hacked off in patches, shorn above her ears. Her money was gone; not a halfpenny to bless herself with. The month was now November, and the moon small and peevish: a copper coin lightly silvered, a counterfeit light.

nine

Mary said, through her bruised mouth, "It was not Bride. Indeed not." Her eyes were cried to slits. She told a tale of being locked in a cellar.

Said Claffey, "Bride Caskey is the cellar queen."

But Mary said, no, she was in a cellar by herself. Till she was starved two days, and would then beg food from anybody. Of what next occurred, she would not speak. Only of a swat in the mouth for insolence, and that came later. She had lost her grip on the passage of hours and days, a faculty that the men had always envied in her, and she seemed to have forgotten certain words and common expressions of her native tongue, so that they were forced to speak to her in a mixture of two languages, which stuck in their throats and blocked the flow of their thoughts.

Howison comes banging in. What a noisy brute he is! Is it a general rule that the man who has strength and gall to handle the deadweight corpse has not the consideration to tread soft among the living? For now it is always night, it is always night at Earl's Court. Hunter is walking with his taper, up and down the storeys, the animal complaints deafening his ears, and replaying in his head the days of heroic experimentation, heroic anger.

Wullie is poorly, they say. Well, let him. All our family have rotten bones.

"So what is it?" he barks at Howison, his man. "What futility have you brought in now, to stop up my ears with trash?"

"You told me, reverence, to bring you in news of the Giant, Charles O'Brien."

"Him? So what's new?"

"Mr. Harry Graham, who is exhibiting—"

"Cut it short, I know all about that mountebank."

"Mr. Harry Graham has offered O'Brien a go on his Celestial Bed, conception assured. With first-time partner of his choice. Free and gratis, whereas the normal rate—"

"Oh, do away with yourself, Howison. I know the rate. I know the rate for charlatans. I'll tell you, shall I, what it is about Mr. Graham's Celestial Bed that produces its results? 'Tis not the naked nymphs playing string instruments, 'tis not the scented odours of incense nor the ostrich feather fans—"

"Really?" Howison looks keen. "I had not heard of the ostrich feather fans."

Perhaps I embroider, thinks John Hunter: can it be that I, a man bound to fact and observation, embroider the tale?

"It is *not either the ostrich feather fans,*" he says, so loudly as to defeat his own qualms. "It is not crushed roses and strewn petals—there's but one way to put a child into a woman's belly, and that is to deliver the vital fluid to her at the right angle, and keep the jilt with her legs up and resting on her back while nature takes its chance. Now to that first point, the tilting mechanism of Mr. Graham's bed explains its own success, and the second effect—the woman's continued posture—is explained by the soporific odours and the sweet music."

Sweet music. His Anne has composed certain verses: "My mother bids me bind my hair." He had heard the song sung. Come home late, his hands stinging from scrubbing, his eyes stinging from lack of sleep. Coming in, a man to his own hearthside, to find the room a-twitter with excitement at some air set down by a foreigner and interpreted by his own spouse: "Get out! Get away to your own beds! I gave no permission for this kick-up."

The falling silent of the instrument, as if a tense string had snapped. The faces only slightly dismayed; the social smiles, the smiles at odds with the eyes, the hurried removal, the sudden silence, and the cowed servants clearing glasses. Crystal's embarrassed chink; remnants of jellies and mousses scraped quickly away. Anne's head dropped: Anne dumb with suffering. Suffering? What did she know about it? Suppose she had a fistula? Suppose she had an abcess under a molar?

Heroic anger. Heroic experiments. "You remember the grocer's wife?"

Grocer's wife of the City: could not get a child. The woman herself seemingly free from disease, broad in the hip, her complexion bright and fresh, no hint of the dragging backache and the pinched yellow-grey that marks the face of the woman whose ovaries are diseased. Her tongue free too, with a frank account of the marital bed. "From which I deduced, Howison, that the man was not what you'd call a going concern. He'd hardly get within a foot of her without spilling on the linen, her thigh was the nearest—"

"You told me before," Howison said.

"So I spooned in the fluid, man. I spooned it in."

"So you said."

"The child was healthy, and thrives to this day."

"I wonder, did you not. . . . were you not tempted . . ."

It took him a moment to grasp the man's implication. "No, sir," he said calmly. "I am a man as we all are, but I would do nothing to introduce experimental error."

But Howison's very question—for suppose others had been asking it, snorting behind their hands?—had reduced him, when the man went out, to a rocking, silent, temple-bursting fury, his short nails driven into his palms, and rock, rock, rock in his chair, his life at the mercy of any imbecile who cared to taunt him . . . for yes, some men would have been tempted, seeing her brown eyes and flushed cheeks; some would no doubt have thought, there is a shorter way and more natural, and if this consultation did not do it, a man might take a guinea for the next, and soon the result would be achieved, for a man would know from the very handling of her, the plushness of her skin, her firmess of her limbs . . . but no. It is all very well to put yourself in your own experiment—it is inevitable, really—but it is unforgivable to bypass the proper procedure to get the required result. The child of the grocer's wife was the child of the grocer, and not in any way—as people can see for themselves—sandy, freckled, or short. The gratification from the experimental process far exceeded that from the sexual act. Yet he remembered the question, and the rage: a little something bursting there, in his left temple.

These rages may be brought on by thwarting: or by the mention of low dirty foreigners who come to Britain on purpose to defame its institutions. "What, you don't like this country, sir? Then quit its shores." Never again, for instance, does he wish to endure the purple throbbing agonies that possessed his forehead (both sides) when a colleague of his remarked that "Dr. Jean-Paul Marat, the noted Swiss savant who calls each day at Slaughter's Coffee House . . . Dr. Marat expresses a desire to see your specimens."

"He does, does he?"

"He will wait on you, sir. At any convenient hour."

"Will he so? Marat? See my specimens? I'll shred 'em first. I'll burn down the whole—burn, I say, live and dead—rather than let that damned Wilkite into my premises."

Because he is establishing order. Night by night: skull arrangement. He is beginning to understand hierarchy; and these democrats will play the Devil with it. And especially a man like Jean-Paul Marat, with his five different names, his silver tongue in seven languages, his embossed certificates, his academic cavils and his snarling quibbles and his slick fingers—what might the man carry away?

"John Hunter, your rages will kill you," his colleague said, expressing a simple truth.

"Yes. And when I am dead, you will not soon meet with another John Hunter."

So: Bitch Mary's tale.

"They had left me the exact time till I was hungry beyond bearing. Another few hours, and I would have been beyond it, God's mercy would have numbed me. I was reduced to meekness and weeping by that hunger, it was agony in itself, but I knew from experience it is a pain which passes. Yet, one may have a piece of knowledge, and be unable to act on it. They plucked me out of the cellar the very moment when my strength was lowest and my need greatest."

"That is how I know it was Bride," Claffey said. "For what nation is more tutored than ours, in the art of hunger and in its science?"

"Ah well," said Joe Vance, "be that as it may, tonight we have men to dine. Mary, my love, I know your clothes are gone, but can you not wrap yourself in a blanket for decency, and then busy yourself? And if you prove yourself useful in putting the place to rights, then tomorrow you will have a skirt and shawl."

"Dress me out of Monmouth Street, would you, Joe? Send the boy Pybus running to the rag-seller, so I can go out again for your purposes?"

"There is some very respectable clothes sold in Monmouth Street," Joe said. "My waistcoat was got there, and you must admit it's very fine."

"Stolen."

"Stolen, so? I bought it in good faith, I will claim my title to this waistcoat in any court in the land. Less of your lip, bitch. The only friends you have are under this roof. Be mindful of it."

The Giant roused from his sleep in the corner. Their speech, he thought, is now a compound of vileness. We abandon our own language because we need extra words, for things we had never imagined; and because there are superfluous words in it, for things we cannot imagine any more. "What men?" he asked. "What men to dine?"

"Slig," said Joe. "You remember hearty Slig?"

"And my brother," Claffey said eagerly. "Constantine Claffey, as he is known at Clement's Inn. Which is where he lodges."

"Which is a midden," said the Giant. "Have I not been all about those parts? It is a midden and a criminal haunt and packed to the gills each split-up low deceiving house and alley with foot-pads and coiners and runners of poor women, with uncertificated pox-doctors and cat-gut spinners, with tripe-merchants and rumour-mongers and rabbit-breeders and slaughterers of the peace of the Lord. Why must your brother lodge there, Claffey? Could he not come here to us at Cockspur Street?"

"He may do that yet," Claffey said.

"As for the man you call Slig—does he not keep that infamous cellar where we lodged when we were freshly arrived?"

"By the dripping blood of Christ!" Vance said. "I am sick of your verbiage. Slig is a sworn brother of mine. Slig gave you straw and a shelter for fourpence. Infamous cellar? It was a usual kind of cellar. I tell you, O'Brien—it was good, of its kind."

"Sick of my verbiage?" the Giant said. "Sick of my stories, also?"

"I leave them to the brutes that want soothing."

"Sick of my person, perhaps, tired of my height?"

"Well," said Vance, sneering, "it doesn't seem as if your height is very remarkable after all. Considering the new intelligence from Cork, communicated to me only this day and then by Slig himself, which is that Patrick O'Brien is now nine feet tall and will be here inside a fortnight."

"And lodge in Slig's cellar?"

"I doubt it. Slig is taken over as his agent now. He will be finding him a good address and a dozen plump virgins to be shaking out the feather beds. He will be getting a pagoda, which I said all along was what we should have, but oh no, you would set your face against it, advised by some rustic—"

The Giant turned his face away. He closed his ears to Joe. Mary said, "When I was walking the streets, and I no longer knew where I was, nor had I known for some hours, I found myself on a wide square that I thought I should recognise. While I was looking about it, to know where I was—it being then broad morning, and I so ashamed of my state, my rags scarcely covering me—then a carriage came, and a lady called out to me from it. She called to me to run after, and I should have sixpence and my breakfast."

Pybus sucked his teeth. "You should not have so."

"I know I should not," Bitch Mary said. "But can you not recollect, Pybus, that I had been many days without a breakfast, and that the thought of sixpence made me summon my last reserves of strength so I could do her will and trot?"

"Joe commands us," the Giant said, "to cut the verbiage." He imagines words hacked down, like shoots in a tangled thicket: slash and cut, cut and burn.

"And so I will," Mary said. "For I have little more to relate. I came to a great house, and anticipated that I would be ushered into a hall, with candles blazing."

"What, in broad day?" said the Giant.

"It was a dark morning. I anticipated Bruges hangings, and Turkey carpets, and Antwerp silver, but what lay before me was London steel. For instead of any of these things, I saw the stone shelves of a pantry, and my head slammed down, and my hair sheared off, and a penny in my hand, and a crust, and out into the cold among the railings in a yard, and Why, why? And they said, To shore up milady's wig. And I said sixpence and they said yes, sixpence: one penny for you and five pennies for us. We're English and we're entitled, and be glad we've not pulled out your teeth."

Constantine Claffey was such a dandy as you would never think to come out of a thieves' kennel like Clement's Inn. His hair was powdered with a strange bluish powder, so his face looked very very white. His bad teeth were painted, and his large front pasted with fine embroidery and one stain from a dripped boiled egg.

"So you've got an interestin' pig?" he said to his brother, in English. "Shall I see it?"

"Ah," Claffey said. "The pig is only a rumour as yet. It is a topic amongst us. It is under discussion."

Constantine sneered. "So you brought me all the way to Cock-spur Street to view a pig under discussion?"

"It's scarcely a half-mile."

"Yes, yes," Constantine said tetchily. "But I have left projects unsupervised. This is what you don't seem to understand, bro. Time and tide wait for no man. Not at Clement's Inn."

Slig, who had got a couple of drinks in him, seemed less anxious to be away. "Isn't there some story promised?" he said. "Your idiot Jankin was giving out there's some story you don't like to tell, about dwarves. Have you heard of Count Buruvalski? Your man's exhibiting here, less than three foot high. Have you seen him, Charles?"

"May I correct you?" The Giant brought his eyes to focus on

Slig. "The count is not a dwarf. He is a midget. That is different. He is, moreover, a thoroughgoing professional in his line of business. He comes from the land called Poland, where snow is deep and small men are honest. If—Joe Vance—if I should decide to dispense with your services—the count is the man to manage me."

"I said, have you seen him?"

"I have seen him, I have bought him a drink. I have sat him on the counter to drink it, the count and I are"—the Giant overlapped his fingers—"like that."

"Oh dear, oh dear," said Vance. "It's the first I have heard of this, Charlie. I was aware, of course, that the midget was sniffing around."

"But look," said Slig, "I would be obliged if you would get ahead with the story nevertheless, because I always want stories. Any spare you have, O'Brien, I can cost them out, and sell them to Punch and Judy. So, I can give you a shilling for each guinea you make me."

"Formerly my portion," Joe Vance said. He sniggered. "How are the mighty fallen."

"I don't know, how are they?" the Giant said.

"I'm going to have to bring your viewing fee down to a shilling, Charlie, or maybe a ninepence is realistic. Unless trade picks up, or we get Mester Goss's pig over sharpish, or we pitch you into prize-fighting, which you seem to resist. You know yourself, nobody comes to see you regular, these days, except that Scotchman, short feller, the animal-trainer—"

"Hunter," said the Giant. "He wrote down his name for me. He said I should send to him if I was sick. But he says physic is not his line, so I don't know why."

Hunter: he had been twice in the last week. "I know that man," Claffey had said, frowning from the back of the exhibition room. "I seem to recognise the swivel on his nose at the tip there, and his pale eyes. A Scot, unless I am much mistaken." Claffey was always looking for a fight. He would have thrown out any client who he thought gave offence. But the Scot gave none. "Too mean to spare an insult," Claffey said. "But that's his nation."

He looked sideways at the Giant: didn't he say his father came out of Scotland?

"The fellow is mannerly enough," O'Brien said. "So far as it is in him. It is clear that he is gruff, unlettered, rude, whereas I am learned, poetical, and fond of civil company."

Besides, the Giant thought, he is the only one who asks after my health, and listens to the answer. Yesterday, silent and attentive as ever, he had been among the audience, his odd eyes set on Charlie's face, looking looking looking. Afterwards, he stepped up. "How do you, sir?"

"The ache in my bones increases."

"As in mine, sir, as in mine."

The Giant paused. "But you are not growing, sir, are you? Surely you are past that, your age must decree it? That is the cause of my distemper. Giants are not subject to the rules that govern other mortals."

"I had observed that," said the Scot: very dry. "This increase in your stature—do you see a good outcome?"

"In terms of income?"

"In terms of your future, sir."

"What is it to you, my future?"

And then the little man washed his hands together. His face reddened. The Giant said, afterwards, he had never seen a man so moved. "I'd like to see you again," the Scot said. "If I talked to your minder, do you think he'd give me some relief on your fee?"

"What, a discount? I think I'm soon down to ninepence, anyway."

"That's good news."

"Not for me."

"Have you any more signs or symptoms, by the way?"

"What?" said the Giant.

"I mean, do you have any further indispositions?"

"Besides what I told you? Yes, I have. I have griping in my brain and my ears, where language is destroyed by slow attrition day by day; where thought is bombinated, as if my skull were a besieged city."

"Anything more?"

"I sleep now. Many hours in the day. I wake at dawn and hear myself growing, before the noise of the criers starts, and the wheels of carts. In the day the city's noise swamps it, but in the watches of the night you may hear the crack as my bones break free of their moorings, and the slap of the tide beaches against my liver. Mr. Hunter, would you enter into my difficulties? A chair already will not fit me. My tailor has to stand on a ladder. He sends in bills that are insupportable."

"Your agent . . . I am surprised, in the circumstances, that he thinks of reducing your rate. I would have thought, on the contrary . . ."

"I don't grow quick enough for Joe. Patrick O'Brien in Cork is springing up day by day. They say he's nine foot tall and practically embarked."

"Indeed? I shall be most interested to see him. What is his age?"

"Pat? He's a young lad, seventeen or so."

"Healthy?"

"Prime."

"I see." The Scot frowned. "Nine foot, you say?"

"By repute."

"We shall see."

"It appears you are fond of giants, Mr. Hunter."

"Oh, I never miss my chance to view. If the tariff is reasonable."

For the benefit of Slig, whose ignorance of dwarves was deep, they had taken to explanations.

"They are the size of a child of seven," Pybus said. "Their skin is the colour of earth, that is because they live in the earth. Their hair is black when young. Their cloaks are black—"

"Or red," said Jankin.

"—and they wear long smocks so you don't see their duck feet. Some of them have hairy ears—"

"And how do they disguise those?" Slig asked.

"With hats," Jankin said. "They can change a lump of coal to a precious jewel. Can't they, Charlie O'Brien?"

"They make cheese," the Giant said. "They have the art of tending to cattle. There was once a man who had seven white cows, and it was the time of year to bring them down from the mountain to the lush valley grass. But the cows were missing, and though he searched all day he found no trace. That night he went to sleep exhausted, and didn't say his prayers. When he woke the next day—"

"—and still no sign of the cows," said Jankin.

"—he decided he would go on as if he had the cows still, so he milked them, invisible as they were, and he led them to the valley, and he fed them all winter on invisible food. When spring came—"

"You'd wonder where he got the idea," said Slig.

"—when spring came, he drove them once more up the mountain. That night, when it was time for milking, his seven white cows came lowing towards him, and trotting after them, nuzzling their silken flanks, came seven shining white calves."

"If Connor's grandfather had only known," Claffey said, sardonic. "Instead of all the shouting, and the breaking of pates among O'Sheas. If he'd just sat tight, he'd have been a wealthy man."

"Well. There is a lesson to be learned," the Giant said.

"You're too tall," Claffey said, "to be so sententious."

"The lesson is not about getting beasts," the Giant said calmly. "The lesson is about believing that things may be invisible but still exist."

Constantine Claffey stirred the coins in his pocket, smirking greasily at the deep jingle. "I like the evidence of my senses," he said.

"Then you are a foolish fellow, Con. Supposing a mosquito lands upon the back of my hand. What do his senses tell him? Ah, here is a nice even plain, very well to romp upon, I'll tell my friends. Ah, here is nice rich blood, I can take a gallon and tomorrow come back for more, we can drink, me and my wife, we can drink a gallon a piece. Then—*splat.* So where is he now, the wise mosquito?" The Giant grinned. "He has joined a larger reality."

"More dwarves!" Jankin demanded. "I want the servant girl in the forest, freezing and starving as night comes down!"

"By the ghost's waistcoat, you are a nasty piece of work," Claffey said. "You are a kind of apprentice piece for a monkey, are you not, Jankin? When the Giant is the whole ape?"

"I only said," Jankin complained, "I only said she is in the forest, and that's true. I only said her belly's empty, which it is because she's been turned out of her home, and I said she's cold because it's usually at least autumn when this tale takes place."

"So she's walking in the forest," Joe said. "And night's coming down? But I bet she spies a little cottage, eh? With a little light burning?"

"Not yet!" Jankin was anxious. "Before she can spot the light she must wander—many hours—and she is shivering and the cold is fierce, each branch of a tree growing into crystal, and she thinks she will not live till morning, for already the ice is crusting her pale hair."

His head bowed, his voice low, the Giant prompted Jankin. "Think—is the cold her only enemy?"

"By no means—she thinks the wolves will devour her, or the bears." He looked up at Slig. "*Devour* is what we say when we mean *eat,* it is a superior word, more terrifying."

"You are eloquent, Jankin," the Giant said.

"For this is a country where there are still bears."

"I see," Joe Vance said. "But presently, she comes to a little cottage, eh?"

"And knocks at the door," Pybus said. "Timidly. The door is opened by a dwarf and behind him are his six brothers, who are all of them dwarves as well."

"Is she a pretty girl?" Con asked idly.

"I don't know. Is she?" Pybus looked at the Giant.

"Her eyes as blue as the cornflower," the Giant said. He felt he was re-using his encomiums. "Her neck like a swan's on a summer lake."

"Very passable, then," Claffey said. "Allowing for the dirty feet and the mud caked on her."

Pybus touched the Giant's arm. "Take up the tale, Mester."

"You know it," the Giant said. "Tell it yourself." The fact was, it sickened him, the tale of the seven dwarves. He was always trying to think of a different ending to it, but the snag was that it ended in the truth.

"Pybus, you tell it," Jankin pleaded.

Pybus raked his fingers through his hair, thinking. "So she comes in. She comes in and she sees it's a snug little place, a fire blazing and an iron pot over it, and a rabbit cooking in that pot."

"Rabbit!" Jankin was distraught. "It was a fat hen stewing, was what I heard. Charlie—"

"Whatever," the Giant said shortly.

"Am I telling it?" Pybus demanded.

"You're telling it," Jankin said.

"The table is set ready with a basket of bread, the candles are burning, and through a parted curtain she can see another room, where there is a row of beds, dwarves' beds, all heaped with animal skins. So the dwarves take her to the fire and she warms herself. She says, 'My dear sir dwarves, will you let me stay the night, and give me a meal from your pot? For out there in the cold the wolves and bears will eat me.' Sorry. *Devour.* So the dwarves look at each other, and the eldest of them—"

"This is the good bit." Jankin hugged himself.

"—the eldest of them says, 'There is nowhere to sleep but our seven beds, so choose one of us to be your companion.' "

"If I know women," Joe said, "she won't run out into the cold again. She won't put herself to the inconvenience."

"You call a bear an inconvenience?" the Giant asked.

"So she consented: saying, 'Which of you is the eldest?' The eldest brother spoke up. 'I'll share your bed,' she said."

"And will the other dwarves watch?" Constantine Claffey said. The Giant's eyes were rivetted to the egg stain on his waistcoat; did he wear it as a badge of wealth, boasting to his neighbours in Clement's Inn that he could afford to eat?

Joe Vance said, "What if she had a dwarf baby?"

Con said, "It's a surprise she didn't say, 'Pull down your nethers and let's have a swift take on your pricks.' And make her choice so. Or were they dwarf as well?"

The Giant stood up. "A need for air," he advised.

He trod heavily downstairs, pushed open the barrier between himself and the night. Bitch Mary was slumped against the wall, her face turned towards the east. A glint from a lamp cut a gilded slice from her cheek: a Saracen's moon. "You're waiting for a client?" he asked.

"Why not? What's to lose now?"

"Claffey would have wed you. It was the sound of your debt put him off."

"Oh, I've paid it," she said. "By God, Charlie, every farthing."

He climbed the stairs again. The room was clogged with smoke. The fire was almost out. Vance sent to the chandlers for their coal, Jankin carrying it by the half-peck. Sea-coal fire, they called it. It sighed before it crumbled, as if the cold sea's voice were in it. The voice of the boy Pybus ran on, continuing the story. "And all that night, in the dwarf's embraces."

Hunter: that same moon, a dripping sabre-cut, slashing at a window of his town house: shutter closed against it, his feet crossed before a low-slumbering hearth.

They say Wullie's worse. His practice has fallen off altogether. Well, let him. I am now the famous Hunter. What did he ever snare but smart society snatches? Whereas my collection is the envy of every contemporary practitioner of human knowledge.

He is bolted in alone, in his cabinet at Jermyn Street. Anne is below, occupied with strumming and verse. Sound carries faintly, floor to floor; laughter that he does not understand. He pours a dram, though spirits are not his vice, the example of whoopsy-go Buchanan being ever before him. A half-glass inside him, he begins to pick a quarrel with someone who is not there: Wullie, perhaps.

There are some stupid men who believe fish to be deaf. If you have ever taken the trouble to discharge a pistol near a fishpond, you will find the truth is otherwise.

"In the morning, early," said Pybus, "a woman of the next village came by, to sell eggs to the dwarves: for they had no fowl of their own. While she was lifting the cloth of her basket, her eyes were travelling about the house, looking to see how the dwarves lived, so she could carry tales to her neighbours. She peeped through the curtain, and then she saw the girl, rising naked from her bed. At once she—"

"Called her a dirty whore," said Claffey.

"At once she cried out, 'You catering slut—to sell them eggs is one matter, but to sleep with them in their beds'—and when the woman slapped her, the girl cried out, 'I was here, only here, to save my life.'

"After the egg-seller had gone, the cottage would be silent. Sometimes she would shake herself, the girl, as if waking from a long sleep, and move half-hearted to the door. But the eldest dwarf would put out his paw to restrain her, with a word and a look of love, whilst his brothers, their cheerful habit subdued, swept out the house and made the neat beds and peeled vegetables for their dinner. So the light began to fade—for it is autumn, and in the forest—and she said, 'It is too late for me to leave now'—and she felt that she might spend a year or two, winter and spring, in the forest amongst the dwarves.

"But when night fell, they saw the light of torches dance between the trees. They heard the murmur of voices. When they opened the door to a knock, it was the egg-seller that stood there. Behind her were the men of the village, armed with clubs. They dragged out the dwarves into their vegetable garden, and beat them to death, one by one, each dwarf watching the pulping of his brother, and the youngest came last. Then they dug up their vegetables and took them away, to cook in their iron pots. Meanwhile the girl hid in the press, among the clean linen, but then she smelled smoke, and this brought her out; she pitched out of the door, jeered at by the men and women, and punched in the face by the egg-seller, as the flames licked the thatch. They spat at her and shook their clubs, and thrust the burning brands into her face, so that she ran into the forest, screaming, barefoot and without her cloak, until she was lost among the trees, and the night's blackness ate her up."

ten

"Now then, O'Brien," said Joe Vance. "You'll have to get another trade. It's not enough to be tall."

The Giant stretched his hands out before him. They were trembling slightly. He knew his elongation not good news, but he wanted Vance to admire him. "But see, Joe. You've remarked yourself how I extend. Paddy, I'll bet you, cannot top me. Nor will for many a year yet."

"That's all very well, growing and growing. But the public's fickle, and in my opinion it's had its fill." He mimicked the mincing tone of an English-speaking gentleman. "Ooh, giants—giants were last year."

"You mentioned a provincial tour, did you not?"

"Sure, but look at yourself, will you? Huddling by

the fire, your nails not trimmed, your coat not brushed, your hair greased on your head like you'd rubbed it with a rasher—are you a sight to inspire Ipswich? Will they batter the doors down in Bath? Will the burghers of Bristol turn out with a pipe band?"

"It was only a thought," the Giant said, sulking.

"The expense of being on the road, Charlie—I'd have to know it was going to be worth the while. No, what I was thinking . . . have you considered fire-eating? Fire-eating's a fine profession."

The Giant gaped at him. "And why must only I have a profession? Why cannot Claffey?"

"Surely," Joe said, "you would not want the attention taken off yourself? As I understand it, any man with a steady hand and his wits about him can be a fire-eater, but why should Claffey have the glory? Ask yourself."

"I wouldn't mind a profession," Pybus said. "Highwayman would suit me. If I had a horse."

"You could be a footpad," Jankin advised.

"Get out of it," said Joe. "Earn a living by any other means. Or they'll tie your gullet, and you'll morrice on air. Remember the litany of the blind man Ferris?"

The Giant had fallen silent. "I have plenty of money," he said at last. "I have no need to continue here, I am not bound in articles to you or any man. I could return to Ireland as soon as passage can be booked. I could take my sack on my back, and turn up in person on the holy site where Mulroney's once stood."

"I'll tell you your trouble," Joe Vance said. "You drink too much."

Early in November, his followers had been out on the streets throwing squibs and crackers; it was an English custom. "I've never been warm since," Claffey said. There had been fighting afterwards. This was five days after the gentry of Ireland had flitted to their wintering grounds, moving silently, gliding white in the dusk. It is unwise to obstruct them, to walk on their paths, or look at them directly. Their existence depends on tricks of the light, and shadows moving through water; their natural state is shadow. They don't count, don't know the days of the week, and use only wooden implements, distrusting iron and steel. They have children by the basketful, and carry them on their backs. All these gentlefolk are very old.

Constantine Claffey came around from Clement's Inn—the egg-stain still on his waistcoat—to tell them a piece of news. It seemed that Goss's pig had become such a huge attraction to the public of Dublin that some cockalorum magistrate rattled in to break up the show, believing it to be an assemblage for the singing of glory-o songs and fomentation of plots against rich men's hayricks. His sergeants had slapped old Goss around the head and threatened Toby with hanging up and salting. Gathering his belongings and his store of money, Mr. Goss had fled for Chester, but hardly had he disembarked when he was seized by brain fever and expired.

"The murdering bully-boys," Pybus exclaimed. "Them blows to the skull of old Goss was no doubt the direct result of his brain fever."

"The cause," the Giant murmured. "Not the result. And Pybus, *post hoc ergo propter hoc* is a pernicious fallacy to lead along the streets."

"I think you are all missing the point," Vance said testily. "The point is, what has happened to Toby?"

Con, with a heave of the chest: "This melancholy tale I shall relate. Toby mourned for two days by his master's grave, off his swill and giving tongue to porcine bleats. On the morning of the third day, when the nephew of Goss, that resides in Chester, came to tempt the pig into better spirits—why, he found him gone."

"Found him gone," said Charlie. "Now there's another phrase to ponder."

"Will you snick your teeth on your pedantry?" Vance demanded. "And you, Con Claffey—less of your bloody bombast. Where is Toby now?"

Con spread out his fingers. "That is what no man knows."

"Then put a description out," said Vance. "And with it, the word that I, Joe Vance, will pay a—what's the phrase, Charlie?"

"Munificent."

"Ah," said Con Claffey. "What a word to roll upon the tongue!"

"Will pay a munificent reward for said pig or information leading to said pig."

"This mu-un-niff-ee-sensse," said Con. "Will it be all your own work?"

Vance shrugged. "I am but a shilling-in-the-guinea man, as you know. But I am hoping O'Brien will seize this investment opportunity."

The Giant made his decision. "If I am not enterprising, I am nothing. Shake hands on it, Joe Vance. I will invest in the pig."

That night, by way of celebration, they had a few drinks, and the Giant told the tale of Tannikin Skinker.

"She was born in a town on the river Rhine, neither a free Hollander nor a subject of the emperor. Her mother, before Tannikin's birth, was asked for alms by an old beggar woman, but she chased her off. As she scuttled, the crone was heard to mutter, 'Hog by disposition thou art, and thy child shall have hog written on her face.'

"Mistress Tannikin, when her mother bore her, was a very proper baby, except for her snout and bristles. Her family, who were of a wealthy sort, kept her hidden in their dark and panelled rooms, behind the casement . . .

"Panelled rooms, in their tall house: where doors opened to reveal doors opening, where shadows painted themselves in the corners, and the dark oils, framed in the low gleam of scarred gilt, pictured doors opening on doors, and women reading secret letters behind looped curtains."

The Giant paused: he saw Tannikin, a big-boned, likely lass of fifteen or sixteen, her snout pressed to a windowpane, the shutter clipped back one fold; beneath her, far below, the little golden ships passing silently down the Rhine.

"Her mother and father tutored her well, and she became proficient in crewel-work, rhetoric and grammar, the use of the astrolabe and terrestrial globes, together with the transcription of music onto the staff; she also possessed a theoretical knowledge of baking, brewing, and the art of beekeeping. Though she had comprehension of seven languages, her voice was a grunt, and she wore always over her face a veil of black velvet."

Again, the Giant paused. In describing Tannikin he had, he realised, gone far beyond the details given by the pamphleteer who had written her life-story. Honesty drew him back to the brutal facts.

"The old woman was at length discovered and taken up by the magistrate of those parts, but was unable or unwilling to lift the curse she had placed on the family. One fact she did divulge, before they touched the torch to the stake—if Tannikin Skinker obtained a husband, one who would love her in spite of her deformity, then she might be restored to the delights of a human countenance, her snout retracting and her bristles falling away as she first experienced the rite of love."

"A pig-face?" Joe Vance said. "Very piggy?"

"Essence of hog."

"Well, I don't know," Vance muttered. It was as if his manhood were challenged. "Was she rich, there's the point of it. Had she a settlement?"

"Her dowry"—and again the Giant saw the gilded ships, freighted with woolsacks and Flanders hops, with silver looking-glasses, oranges from Sicily, and the fruit of Franconian vines. "Her dowry was . . . munificent. It was . . . ample."

"Then put a bag on her head," Claffey said, "and I'll do the business. Is she still on the market?"

"Mistress Tannikin," the Giant said, "was born in the Year of Grace 1618."

"So?" Claffey said. The almanac was no part of his education.

The Giant continued on. "When this was noised abroad—and there were, as you may imagine, many curious and talkative spectators at the trial of the old witch—the town and even the house of the Skinker family were discovered to the public, and a parade of valiant but impecunious gentlemen besieged the door. They bore hand-coloured illustrations, on vellum, of their armigerous bearings, and in lieu of these, written references from magistrates, ministers of religion, and some in triplicate from the Holy Ghost himself.

"The Skinker family employed the town's best dressmaker and its most applauded coiffeur. They had their dear daughter Tannikin padded with horsehair hips and entrammelled in hooped petticoats, and her sweating pink limbs encased in the finest brocade and sateen; and they persuaded the bespoke hairdresser to pin up and powder her coarse hair according to the best fashion of the time, and then they called for the milliner to deck her with a bonnet that was so beribboned, so decked with fruit and flowers, so embroidered over with every manner of child and beast, that men called it the Wonder of the West."

He paused again. Gone too far with the bonnet, but what did they know of female modes? Gone too far with the Holy Ghost and the suitors, but what did they know of theology, or romance? He pictured Tannikin Skinker, while they tweaked and pinned and powdered her, with her trotter shielding her eyes, afraid to peep: longing again for the comforting dusk of her black velvet mask.

"And yet it was to no avail, any of it. Englishmen came, Frenchmen and Italians, Chinamen and Tartars, yet at the sight of the pig-face of Tannikin, all quailed: all made their excuses: all doffed their bonnets, and sadly took their leaves."

"I'd not have been so precious," Claffey said.

"But Tartars—" said Joe Vance.

Said Claffey, "Tartars are nothing."

"Tartars, I'll have you know, are very fine trick-horsemen. I wish I could get a Tartar."

"And so she lived to the end of her days," the Giant said. "Her father and mother died . . ." It must have been so, but he had had only just realised it. "Her father and mother, who tutored her in the liberal arts, and who would have given their whole fortune to have discovered to their sight her true, human face. Then poor Tannikin was alone, behind the shutters peeping out to see the river run, and the fashions change, and her lovely bonnet grow into ill-repute—ever willing, till she reached advanced years, to entertain a suitor who had heard of her but lately . . ."

Until her servants died, he thought, the old servants who had been used to her, and there was no one to shine the silver bowl in which she used to eat her swill, and no one who could bear the sight of her face, no one who would read her a sermon or bring her Holy Communion, or stoke up her fire when the nights were sharp. "Mistress Tannikin Skinker," he said, "lived a long time, in humility and solitude. As such creatures always do."

Pybus, looking up, thought he saw a tear on the Giant's cheek; but the light was fading, and appearances can deceive.

"It's a pretty enough tale," Con Claffey said, yawning. "But I would sooner have the coal-heavers strike, and how Murphy and Duggan were brought to the fatal tree."

The Giant thought, there are trees in worlds unknown to Claffey and his ilk, that bear fruit and flowers on their branches at one time.

"And come to think of it," Claffey said, "I would sooner have a drink at the Talbot in Tyburn Road. Are you coming, brother?" He nodded back towards the Giant. "Another you would do well to add to your agenda is the Irishmen's gallant charge on the butchers of Clare Market."

"Why were they charging on the butchers?"

"Because they made an effigy of the sainted Patrick, and were burning it on a great fire, and singing songs."

"Did they so?" Pybus shouted. "By God, I'd have charged myself."

Said the Giant, "Pybus, these days you'd charge if a cabbage leaf blew across the street."

Said Constantine, "We stripped them flesh from bone."

At Jermyn Street, alone and in the dark, John Hunter is juggling with the metacarpals of an ass.

Soon, from the Talbot and the Swan with Two Necks, from the Quiet Woman and the Three Keys, there came a flood of false intelligence concerning pigs; and worse, a steady procession of handlers and herders, dragging up Piccadilly with dreary porkers on chains. One of them was not even a pig, but a bulldog shaved; which offered, the Giant said, a measure of the English intelligence. Said Pybus, "I wonder what became of the pig from the cellar, you remember, Charlie, the pig that was the blind man's hope?"

"Gone to rashers," the Giant said: rashers long consumed.

Pybus crossed himself.

Joe Vance stood out in the yard, mopping his brow at the parade of gross rolling flesh. "It's well-known," he said, "that Mester Goss's pig is a slick black pig, that was under training with Goss—God rest him—since he was a yearling, and is not now above three years old. Why do they waste my time with these impostures?"

He mopped his brow again. "An agent's work is never done."

The Giant said, "What about the Scotchman? The little animal-trainer? Is it not likely that he may have some information? He is no doubt able to write, and may have provincial connections he could consult."

Joe rubbed his chin. "We have not seen him lately. Did he not leave his card on you, Giant?"

The Giant said, "It is among my effects."

Howison has been reading a book about werewolves. By and large, the werewolves of France are malign and drooling, scarlet-toothed predators on the meek lamb Christ and the sheep who are his people; whereas the werewolves of Ireland are heroes and princes, cast into melancholic lycanthropia by ancient curses, condemned for seven years to their grey hairy hides and their glinting eyes, to raw meat and dread of flames. Yet sometimes they are still Christians under the pelt: witness the Werewolf of Meath, who besought a travelling priest to bring the last sacraments to his dying wife, and peeled back her skin to show her human nature. Another brute creature—a wolf indeed—terrorised the Massif Central, in 1764, attacking grown men and causing fifty deaths. One small boy who was badly frightened but not eaten by this wolf stated that it had a row of buttons on its underside. The louche reported that it came to town when it needed to visit its tobacconist; the pious stated that it came to town when it wished—being a talking wolf—to confess its sins.

And receive absolution?

The English do not have werewolves. For them, you're either one thing or the other.

The mornings were icy now, and for the first time in his life the Giant began to feel the cold. Aching and snuffling, he brooded over the smoking fire; and when Claffey said to him, "Coming to the Scotchman then?" he looked up, lethargic, and shook his head.

"Hunter frightens me," he said. "When he laid his hand on me to feel my pulse, he felt right through to my bone."

"Suit yourself," Claffey said. "You look like a sick dog."

At Jermyn Street, the door was opened by a hulking man they had never seen before. "Yes?" he barked. "Are you an experiment?"

Claffey did not understand him at all, but he thought a shake of the head might be safest.

"Then why have you come around here by broad daylight? Where's your sack?"

"Our sack, sir?"

"Where's your deceased, you dimwit. Where's your corpse?"

"We are still living, mester," said Jankin.

"We have come about the animals, sir," said Pybus.

"Oh." The big man let his breath out, and looked at them less hostile. "Animals is sent to Earl's Court, that's where Mr. Hunter keeps his animals. What have you got? Alive or dead?"

The Irishmen looked at each other. Claffey's feet twitched, in spite of himself, they clearly thought he should cut and run. But Jankin said, disconsolate, "So we cannot see their tricks then?"

"Tricks?" the man said. "God blast you, we're not a circus."

"Look," Claffey said, "it seems to me there's some misunderstanding, sir." He reached into his pocket, and pulled out a piece of paper scribbled over. "The little Scotchman gave this to our giant. It's his name written down, I believe."

"Yes," said the man, staring. "This is a page from the sacred pocket book of Mr. John Hunter."

"That's the fella. A twist to his nose, and his shoulders up under his ears, and bristles on his cheeks."

"Why, you insolent rogue," the man burst out. "I'll pull out your kidneys for you."

Just then they heard a sharp voice from the interior of the house. "Howison, who is it out there?" The Scotchman appeared, wearing a long smock over his coat; on the front of it, exactly where Constantine Claffey had his egg-stain, there was a particle of something ruddy and gelatinous.

"Bunch of paddy thatch-gallows," Howison replied. "I'll boot 'em, sir."

"No, wait. Aren't you fellows the Giant's crew? Haven't I seen you with Charles Byrne?"

"That's us," replied swagger-boy Pybus.

A look of effortful geniality spread itself at once over the Scotchman's face. "And how's your big fella today?"

"Like a sick dog, sir," Jankin said. "Ain't he, Francis Claffey?"

"Hm," said Mr. Hunter.

"Sits by the fire and does naught," Jankin added.

"I see. Now then, gentlemen"—Mr. Hunter plunged his hand under his gown and fished about. Pybus braced himself, wondering would he pull out a knife; he distrusted the nature of the stain on his clothing. Mr. Hunter's flat palm came out with three-halfpence on it. "Oh dear, Howison. I shall have to step out to a patient and earn a guinea. How is it I'm down to this?"

"You purchased those newts. An impulse, sir."

"True, I had forgot the newts. Well, gentlemen, take the will for the deed. I would have seen you right if I could. Do you ever take a drink at the Crown, on Wych Street?"

"We might," said Pybus.

"If you see my man Howison in there, he'll treat you all round. Howison, take notice of these men. They and we shall have some dealings before many months have passed."

"It's a mystery walking," Pybus said, as they set off back to Cockspur Street. But by the time they got there, Joe Vance had solved it for them. "Slig's been round, he put me wise. The man is no animal-trainer. He is what they call in England a crocus."

"Which is to say?" asked the Giant.

"Which is to say, he is a surgeon. He cuts for the stone and takes off green legs. He is one of those anatomies of whom you have been singing."

"His man offered to pull my kidneys out," said Pybus. "I took it for banter."

"We'd best stay away from him," Jankin said. "And his man Howison. And the Crown on Wych Street."

Vance gawped. It was the longest speech he'd ever heard Jankin make, and it was stuffed with sense. But Claffey said, "He swore he'd treat us all round, and I suppose his drink's as good as any other man's, crocus or no crocus." Claffey was out late these nights, scouring for Bride Caskey. No matter what Mary might say, he was convinced that it was she who had despoiled his darling.

Mary went out on her own account these nights. "I have nothing left to lose, so I try to make gains," she explained. She was angry when they tried to hold her back. "I too want money in my pocket. I want a sack like the Giant's. But I know I shall be dead before I get it."

Mary's hair seemed to have darkened; she looked older, and wilder. The Giant thought of the eldest brother, the eldest brother of the dwarves. Of his word, his look of love. It was these things detained the maiden in the forest. He said nothing to Mary. Let her go: as well be outside in the disaster, as inside, locked up with it.

Each night the rooms grew smaller, at Cockspur Street. There was a scraping noise inside his chest. "You could do with a dose of physic," Vance suggested, but he said no, no, keep away from physic, and keep away from the crocus. God bless us, he said. St. Comgall keep us. Mary neglected the scrubbing. The rooms grew fusty. One afternoon he burst open the nailed-shut window. A black north wind rattled the sashes.

Christmas came on. The peck was getting rougher. They dined on a sheep's head boiled, and called it a banquet; most nights it was bad bread and loblolly.

"Open your sack, Giant," young Pybus groaned. "Let us have a slice of ham, as we did in former days. Let us have seed cake."

"I will open my sack for Toby," the Giant said. "For no project else."

"Not even eating?" said Pybus. "Oh, pitiful."

"The devil of a pig," said Slig, as slowly he stirred his turnips and gruel, "the devil of a pig is, will it sit in a chair? Now, Constantine Claffey has heard of a bear that's for rent—"

"I am not parting with my money for a bear. A bear is disagreeable to me."

"But Charlie, you're not listening. The fact is, you can get a bear and shave it. Then you put a bonnet on it and a gown, and its face peeps out shy and lovely—and you must put gloves on it and pad the fingers."

Said the Giant, "You'd think grown men would have better things to do."

"Then you drape its chair very full, so that a little lad can hide under. You cry it out as 'the Pig-Faced Lady'—we can call her Tannikin if you like—and when the folk have paid their money, you ask it a question, such as, 'You are a lady of Limerick, I believe?' Then the boy pokes it from beneath with a stick, and Tannikin goes grunt. Then you say, 'How do you feel, that people describe you as the Pig-Faced Lady?' And the boy pokes it twice, and it gives two grunts, very angry, and so you pretend to be the soul of consideration, and you say, 'We'll not talk of it,' and the boy tweaks the bear, and she gives a little soft groan, as if she were pacified."

"It seems to me," the Giant said, "that the beast's repertoire would be limited. I cannot imagine you would attract more than a low class of gawper."

"It's a clever thing," Slig insisted. "I've seen it done."

From their first visit to the Crown in Wych Street, the boys came home slewed and rolling. Constantine Claffey was sick on his waistcoat, but he wore it next day just the same. "When they go to the tavern these days," Joe Vance explained, "they call the first bevvy their quencher. Then it's their rouser, then it's their cheerer. After that they don't bother giving it names."

Joe was a leaner man these days, and his eyes were mild as he sat by the fire with his book on his knees, and gazed into the middle distance. One day, when the Giant came home, he found that Joe had sold the siskins. Seated on the chair with the dint in its back, the Giant wept.

eleven

The landlord Kane called on them, in response to complaints. "Heavy treading," Kane said, "that's what I hear."

"God damn," said Claffey, "he's a giant, what do you expect, fairy footsteps?"

Kane glared at Claffey. "Wrap it, skin-pate, or you're out on your ear."

"Claffey does have a point," said Joe.

The Giant lay on his back on the floor and pretended to be asleep. He gave false snores.

"Them people below pay good money," Kane said, "clients of mine. They say the freak is walking all day and night."

"It is called pacing," Joe explained. "He is restless and ill-at-ease. He is homesick, I think."

"You ought to sell him," Kane said. "What's the good now? All novelty's worn off. You could hire him out as a whole gang of labourers."

"He'll not do manual work," Joe said. "Not that he is too proud, but he says his muscles are tearing off the bone."

"Have you ever considered you could swap him?"

"I'd certainly swap him for a sapient pig, if one could be got."

"I'll tell you what's a good act," said Kane. "Tibor the Terrible Tartar."

"Tibor," said Slig. "I know the lad. His father's from Cork."

"Nothing between the ears," said Kane, "but will bestride two horses at once, standing up, and catch an orange on a fork."

"And is he for sale?"

"Only that one of the steeds is coughing and ready for the knackers, so he's looking for finance, cut somebody in on a percentage. Think about it." Kane looked down at the Giant. "What's that his head's resting on?"

"His money bag."

"By the lights!" said Kane.

"There is one that still likes Charlie," said Jankin, piping up from the corner.

"And who's that?"

"The crocus," said Jankin. "Anatomy."

"Which anatomy?"

"Hunter," Joe Vance said.

"Hunter, is it?" Kane rubbed his chin. On his way out he carefully inspected the chair with the dint. He frowned over it, wobbled it from side to side. He left, increasing their rent as he did so.

"So how was the Crown?" the Giant asked, a week later. "It's your only haunting-ground, now."

Pybus slapped his chest. "Brave and bloody," he said. "We're singing a song called 'Sandman Joe,' we don't understand the words but it's very vulgar, an ill-used horse is in it so Jankin went out of the room."

"And who taught you this song?"

"Mester Howison, the surgeon's man. He will drink with Irish, there's no harm in him. Bully Kane was there, our landlord, and Con Claffey, and Bully Slig."

"Oh yes?"

"Mester Howison asked after you," said Claffey. " 'How is Charles Byrne these days?' was how he put it."

Nights sharp as a scalpel. Spring frozen, sap locked into the trees. Wullie Hunter has gout, an ailment he despises. Day and night he is in pain. The Giant thinks, if I die, how will they bury me? The ground is harder than a bailiff's heart.

Wullie feels, within himself, an unaccustomed heaviness. He would mention it to his brother, if they were on terms.

The Giant says, "Joe, whenever I pass a stairhead, I feel an attraction to fall down it."

Bitch Mary comes home with her face beaten in.

Joe says, "These are not the days we have known."

John Hunter keeps to his routine. He rises in the dark, and rinses his mouth in water that has stood since the night before. He pisses—an activity less painful than formerly—and rubs grit out of his eyes. He strokes his bristling chin, he scrubs his white freckled body and dabs it with his linen towel. He begins dissecting before six, and the frigid dawn peeps in at his indecencies, at his scoured-raw hands hauling bowel, at his excised bladders and hearts thrown in a dish.

At nine, he breaks off for breakfast. Gooseberries in a mutton tart remind him of eyes rolling on the slab. Eyes reminds him of optics, optics reminds him of that Swiss devil Marat with his increasingly twisted-up and mad set of theories about the nature of light. Where is Marat this morning? Hunter stops eating, and starts imagining. His pulse shoots up. He pushes his pie aside. Remembers brother James, jiggling like a half-disjointed idiot on the stool in the kitchen at Long Calderwood; and how sister Dolly tenderly placed an extra log on the fire, at the sight of him. James with his cheeks blazing, his cold sweat, his bones fighting out through the skin. Marat reckoned he could cure tisick and bone rot, cure the pox too, and if he could do either or any it was from gab gab gab, his continental blawflum and the gradual, creeping, magnetising power of his gold-striped eyes—gentle as sin, God rot him.

Put off his breakfast by thoughts of Marat and other malpractitioners, he would receive his patients. He would go on his rounds, and dine at four. He put little on his plate, he drank no wine. (Wine, and even more, spirits, disposes to springing skull-splitters, headaches so vast, so penetrating, so mobile, that he feels some vast satanic fisherman has gaffed him through the hard palate and is working him to land.) He would leave the table as soon as good manners allowed, and go to lie down for an hour; but this time for recuperation, if he had dined too heavy, was filled with the heaving spectres of democrats, and the dead. When he rose, he would dictate case-notes, or write them up himself. He would prepare a lecture, or deliver one. By twelve midnight, the household was in bed; and he alone, walking till one or two, listening to the clocks as they struck across the city.

Five years ago—he consults his notebooks, and sees it was five years ago now—he took a turn for the stranger—his routine broken, his patients deserted and referred elsewhere, while for ten days he lay suspended it seemed on air, his body spinning, faster and faster spinning. This was stage one: waking in the night, to this gyroscopy.

Stage the second: he is two feet long.

Stage third: John Hunter's feet lost. He can move them, but they are someone else's. He can't claim ownership, despite the motive power.

In this stage, he can't stand the light. They close the shutters but he begs to be blindfolded; not that anyone can understand his speech. A noise makes him scream: any noise, the hooves of horses clip-clop in Jermyn Street, the buzz of a fly blunting its head in the corner, or Anne's voice calling out, "Oh, the post's come." The harpsichord-clavichord-any-bloody-chord, hammer or quill on string, they hurt his viscera, pluck liver and lights, pluck and plick, conducing to shriek, and a sort of terrible silent sobbing inside himself, which occasionally lurches up into his throat and batters at the back of his clenched teeth: in which he's saying, Bring me Mesmer, bring me Marat, bring me any bleeding bollocking quack you care to name—pay him to stop it, stop it happening, stop it happening now.

Stage fourth: after ten days, he's out of bed, leaning on an arm. He claims kinship with his feet—he knows, intellectually, that they belong to him—and he accepts that he has returned to his true size. Colour is unreliable; the fire burns purple in the hearth, and no one will explain why this is so. There is no centre in him, so he can't balance. His hands swim in dislocating space. They feel their way towards nothing. If he wants to put his hand on an object, he has swiftly to calculate the distance, and watch his hand as it moves. If he wants to plant his feet, he has to predetermine where they'll rest, heel and toe. It's as if something's gone inside, as if his spring were broken.

And now, in times of violence and cold weather, he sometimes feels the wash of nausea, sees through slitted eyes the city jaundiced, which he takes to be a warning, for this yellow pigmentation stained his world for ten days before the strangeness and the pain arrived inside him.

After this, Anne persuaded him to Bath. He drank the waters. He still believed he would die. He slept lightly and had dreams, in which blood ran down the walls, and it was his. Returning to London, he went to the meeting of a committee, at St. Georges'. The agenda swam before his eyes. The faces around him adopted singular arrangements, eyes on top of nose, nose floating off to the left, teeth detaching themselves and falling with a soundless clatter to the table top. The chairman rapped on this table top with his pencil. "Come on, John Hunter. Keep up."

John Hunter is nervous of speaking in public. Standing before his awed, gaping students, his thoughts disorder, slip sideways, and snag themselves. He needs thirty drops of laudanum, before he can stand up to it like a man. Otherwise, what happens? His scribbled-over papers fumble and flit to the floor. *Did I drop them?* He must apologise, recapitulate: "I'll start all over again."

Long after midnight, Pybus went into the yard for air. Fumes of spirits went before him, gusting on the night. There was frost in the air, and the frost killed the fumes; he stood breathing quite sweetly. He shifted his feet on the stones; since he came to England his feet were more calloused than ever, but the hard skin did not keep out the chill. Vance, at the Giant's behest, had provided them all with leather shoes, but Jankin had thrown his overboard, when they were at sea. He believed they were a torment or some kind of shackle; and yet he, Pybus, was resolved to persevere—except when he was in private—because both the Giant and Joe Vance insisted that the constant wearing of shoes was a mark of the high life, and after all, Pybus, they would say to him, your daddy wore them, your grandaddy wore them, it is only in your own poor generation that you are forced to be so closely acquainted with mother earth. The Giant himself wore great boots, which he said were made from the skin of forty calves, and it was the work of Pybus to polish them with a rag; but by and by, he thought, this task will pass to Jankin, and I will go on to greater things.

So, standing as he was, the smoke of evening fires drifting around him, he heard a sound, a grunting, rutting sound. He thought, it is the pig! His ears were attuned that way; all of them, constantly, were expecting Toby Goss, the slick black genius from Dublin. His head swivelled in the direction of the noise, and then he began to walk.

Beside the house was a little passage. It led him to a back court, very cramped. Very stinking, and dark shapes moving in it, confused animals, two heads and a heaving back. His heart came into his mouth, for he remembered that creature they had seen in Ireland, running in the ruins: half-hound, half-babby. He stepped back into the passage, and crossed himself. At that moment the moon—so soiled, so grounded in puddles—came sailing high above the buildings.

By its gentle light, he was able to separate the animal shapes into human form. He saw that on the ground was Bride Caskey, and Claffey was on top of her. He saw that Claffey's buttocks were white, and meagre in form though energetic in action, and that the woman's eyes were closed and that she was bleeding from her mouth. Her kerchief was pulled off her head and lay beside her, lifting in the wind; the merest inch was trapped beneath the boot of the man Slig, and Pybus watched it flapping, fighting to be free. Slig was unbuttoned, and he held his member in his hand, rubbing the tip and watching and listening as the woman's skull tapped the cobbles, tip, tap, tip, tap, with every lunge of Claffey.

Something touched Pybus. He almost screamed. A human shape fell back into the darkness of the passage; it was Bitch Mary. "Pybus?" When she raised her skirts, her white thighs shone like two slivers of moon. "Be quick," she said. "Here, against this wall. I must get my own baby, wizened or yellow or dwarf, to replace the babies hanged."

Pybus opened his breeches. He looked back over his shoulder. Surely by now they were forcing a dead woman? There was a sort of blot on the cobbles by Caskey's head, but he did not want to think about its nature. Mary put her hand out and yanked at his cock. He gave a little yelp, so small—saw her eyes blaze up, and then her fist came out of nowhere, and his nose spewed blood, and it was dark.

The Giant lay, bug-bitten. His blanket covered him no more than a handkerchief would cover an ordinary man, but something seemed to have got into the weave, into the knitting of it, so that it fratched against his flesh, and he thought by morning he would be rubbed raw in patches. The city's bells tolled: two o'clock. He realised he was alone, except for Jankin—who had never made a success of sleeping in a bed—curled whimpering in the corner.

He rose. He stretched himself, not upwards but outwards; he did it cautiously; but still the walls skinned his knuckles. He pulled on his breeches and shirt, and threw the blanket around his shoulders. "Hic," said Jankin in his sleep. "Hic." And, "My eyes are blinded."

Down and out into the street. Down the back alley, towards the noise that had cracked the eggshell of his rest.

Pybus lay like a landed fish on the cobbles. The girl stood over him. She was angry, broad-shouldered and set, her hands on her hips. "I have a disease," she said. "I have taken a dislike to this ape here, and I meant to pass it on to him before I die. But then, I could not. And there was nothing for it but knock him down."

"You should not defame apes," the Giant said. "And Pybus is only a boy."

"I am only a girl." Mary sucked at her knuckles; they had met the teeth of Pybus, on the way to his nose. "They have slaughtered Bride," she said, "Claffey and the man Slig."

The Giant took a step, and stood over Bride. Her face was a vacancy; everything had gone out of it. He put his hand under her head, and felt his palm sticky, blood and brain. "Murder is their nature," he said. "Just as my nature is giant, and Joe's nature is agency."

"And mine is street molly and tib, it is Covent's Garden nun. Nature cannot be helped, I suppose. It cannot be prayed against. I ply my trade on my back; I am a stargazer."

"Where can we take her?" the Giant said. "I am not familiar with the burial customs in these parts."

"Some midden or tip," Mary said. "It's the fate of our nation."

There was a soft *a-hem* from the shadows. It was Joe Vance, coming home late. "Mr. Hunter would like her, I think. She's very fresh. She'll go to waste, otherwise. What's the point of that? I ask myself."

"They say," said Mary, "that the road from Ireland to heaven is a beaten track, worn smooth with the feet of all who tread it; but the road there from England is grassed and flowery, for it is walked but once in a decade. I understand this now, as formerly I did not."

The Giant looked down at Joe Vance. "I cannot alter your mind, Joe. You are the agent and prince of us all. But I will not be accomplice to the cutting up of Bride Caskey. Murder has been done; it is enough. If you wish to sell her to the man Hunter, you must hire a handcart, for I will not be the one to carry her to that filthy fate."

"Very well," Joe said shortly. "You'll have the grace to place her under cover. It's coming on to rain."

The thin night drizzle fell on his blanket as the Giant stooped over Bride. Her body seemed half the size of the living woman, as if Claffey and Slig had systematically reduced her in some type of bone-crusher. "Heavy as a bird," he said. "Heavy as a bag of feathers. It only amazes me that Constantine Claffey was not engaged in this piece of desperation, for there's another raider of the high hills of hell."

He laid Bride under the jutting eaves, and threw his blanket over her face. It can't itch her now, he thought. He picked up Pybus and carried him up to their room, where he washed his face and so roused him: to face the broken day, to feel his tender gums, to take his split—by eleven that morning—for watching the murder of Caskey and saying naught; Joe came in brisk and cheery, the guineas from Howison in his hand, and moved about the room quite liberal: "A shilling for you, Pybus lad. A shilling for Mary, and a shilling for Charlie O'Brien."

The Giant threw his shilling on the boards. Joe picked it up again. "Suit yourself," he said.

"A shilling for Claffey . . ." But then he thought better of it. "After all, Claffey had the gratification," he said.

Claffey was hacking at a lump of cheese. His appetite was excellent. "Bloody buggering scheme of yours," he said, "to take the bitch to the anatomy—a stroke of brilliance, Joe. At least we got some cash out of her carcase. Plus, when cut up into little bits, she won't be rising again, on the last day or any other bloody day, to torment a good man with her witticisms and sell young girls into sin."

Joe—his expression wondering—handed Claffey the shilling. God help him, the Giant thought; all my stories have not prepared Joe for this extremity, and nor has his book about the prince. He said, "Gentlemen, I shall treat you one and all. Tonight I open my purse, and we will carouse at the Black Horse."

"We'd sooner the Crown," said Jankin, but Joe swatted him and said, "Don't put the man off his pleasures."

All of them were grinning. "I'm thinking," the Giant said, "you've been too much at the Crown lately."

Diversion was his idea.

Wullie has shrunk, was John's first impression; the deathbed wiseacres remind him that this was quite a usual misperception. He thinks of the diminutive Irishwoman brought only yesterday, raped and half-throttled and bashed to death—her skull beaten in, against a wall, he supposed, or on the ground. The Giant's band of mad Irish had fetched her, and Howison knew better than to ask questions: only take in fresh supplies, welcome while they are supple, and get them on the table.

William had begun to complain of his symptoms on fifteenth day, third month, Year of Grace 1783. He, John, had made an annotation in his book. Thursday, twentieth day, William had got out of his bed to give a lecture. He was brought back to his house in a state of collapse. Twenty-second day of this month, an incident occurred in the night; let us say the rupture of a small vessel, let us say some bleeding into a small space, let us say some leakage, let us say he's a goner.

After this, they send for John, and he comes, of course. Whoever lives longest will win the contest. If he is honest with himself—and he is always that—he will say their quarrel did not so much touch on the structure of the placenta, as it touched on who should take credit for the work of discovering about it. For he thought Wullie had beaten him out of glory, as Wullie often did; he humble, meek, and useful, and Wullie your high-society dandy. But what does it matter now—your man collapsed among his pillows, white as thin paper, crying.

March 29: the spring long in coming: buds sealed on the trees still, and Wullie ebbing visibly. He speaking, he's saying, "John, when you come to it, as I have, as I know I have—when you come to it, it's not hard to die."

He leans forward, and with a handkerchief dabs a spool of dribble from his brother's lower lip.

Some lawyer of William's is sitting beside the bed. He leaps up and flitters by John's elbow, as he crosses the room to stare down into the street. "He's left you naught," he says. "Dear Mr. Hunter. Don't think it."

"I wanted naught," John says. His voice rasps in his throat.

William is still calling out to him: believe it, John, believe it, dying's not so hard.

Tears are blurring his eyesight. He stands with his back to the bed, so as not to show them. He says, "It's poor work, brother, if it comes to that."

At the Black Horse that night, there was a scene the Giant had not prepared for. Joe Vance, his face white, his little hands moving up and down. "For I cannot abide," he said. "I cannot bide more."

"But Vance, my agent," the Giant said. "For grief's sake, don't abandon me."

"Not at this juncture," said Constantine Claffey; who had become—the Giant did not know how—part of his treat.

"I can no longer stay in this town," said Vance.

"Ah, come, come," said Claffey. "Dear Joe, you are drink taken. Tomorrow you will think again."

"Tomorrow I will not," said the wrecked and weeping agent. "I must remove or die. I cannot be here in this city. The streets are thronging with opportunity, the stones running with gore. I have read the bible of the strangling necks, their handbooks and their lore, and I feel the pull of England's fatal cord: Jack Ketch is coming for me. For Ketch is what they call the hangman, he has but one name, and that one is not his own."

"Jack Ketch, to my knowledge," drawled Constantine, "has been dead these many hundred years."

Said Pybus, "It is what he saw at the puppet show. At Bartholomew. He is unhinged by it."

"Unhinged?" said Claffey. "He is a gate flapping in the gale."

John Hunter is sitting in the dark, among his skulls. He's knuckling his own head. He's saying, Not hard to die. He's saying, Poor work if it comes to that. He's saying, Oh God blast. And Wullie with more work in him, years more work yet. And he's saying,

I'm sure I'll never die: except in a fit where the world looks yellow, in a fit where upright objects slope, when the pain in his chest so starves his brain that nothing filters through but narrow and yellow and slanted: where he begins violently to daydream, and the world in those dreams is close and full of texture and the snuff of death and its very colour, which colour he now knows, and different God damn me from the blue of Wullie's face, as different God damn me as the lark from a starling.

When they woke up next morning, Joe Vance was gone.

"You had to expect it," Claffey said. "It was a case of blind panic. My brother says he's seen it before, in men who've been in London six months or a year. A sort of addling begins in their heads, a scrambling, he calls it, in the senses—they cannot help it, but the next thing is they are cut and run."

Pybus shook his head. Poor old Joe. They did all, truly, commiserate with him.

One snag. This was not discovered till the Giant rose, muzzy-headed and nauseous, sometime after eleven. Along with Joe had gone the Giant's bag of money, seven hundred in pounds sterling.

"I'll scour the bugger," Claffey said. "I'll scour him out. I scoured for Caskey and I found her and I beat her sodden skull in. I'll do the same for Vance. There's not a ditch in this ville where he can hide from me. There's not a hole so low that my eye won't be in it."

"Why break sweat?" said his brother Constantine. He dusted some debris from his waistcoat. "Think about it, bro—what does it matter to you that the Giant's money's gone? 'Tisn't as if you were seeing the colour of it."

"That's true, I suppose," Claffey said.

The Giant lies on his back on the floor. Their legs weave about him, so do their verbals. He puts his hands over his ears to stop the sound, but to do that he has to take them away from his eyes, and then light filters in. He closes his lids hard, he screws them down. But all the same the red winter's day nips under his skin, and steals his blackness.

Let me be blindfolded, he thinks. He remembers Jankin's dream, out of which the idiot spoke a line of verse: *my eyes are blinded.*

He thinks, *my speech is silent.* The verse is the mother's lament, as Herod's hangmen come for the babies, to gibbet them by their doors. *My heart's a blood-clot.*

Let us say we reverse time. Suppose the Holy Innocents grow up. Suppose they grow up and one becomes a horse-thief and another a bigamist, one tells lies in the journals and another fires his neighbour's barn, say one becomes a soldier, say one becomes a whore: say they trample through Palestine, conflagrating, confabulating, mad and dirty as Uxbridge brick-makers, say one becomes an idiot, and one becomes a king.

Where's your Herod then?

The Giant's ribs heave, up and down, up and down.

Men staring down at him. Strangers, in all but name. And estimating. Sizing him up. Selling by the inch.

"So, now," said Con Claffey smoothly, "you can work the freak as he should be worked. Never mind the beau-monde and their half-crowns. Half-crowns are all very well, but there is a limited quantity in circulation. All the society people in this town have already viewed your giant. Open him up now to the plaudits of the multitude. Ask them but one penny. Those pennies will soon add up."

"It will be a great while before they add up to the size of the pile Joe Vance ran away with."

"And so? You can diversify. For now that Vance has gone, you're cock of the walk, I'd say. The boy and the addle-wit will do what you say, and as for the brute, dope him, Fran, if you must—though it strikes me he's tractable enough."

"Yes. He's docile these days. And what can he do without his money? Used to threaten to flounce off to Mulroney's, but where can he flounce now?"

"Where at all?"

"He's to be my creature," Claffey gloated. He stared down. "You're my creature, Charlie O'Brien, and I'm your only agent now."

"So what you do, you go to Slig, say, convenient cellar wanted. Only condition, it must be deep enough to let the brute stand up and show off his attributes, get him crouching low and it misses the whole point. A cellar then, deep and dirty. One penny to come down the steps and view. They'll flock, brother. Every punk in England."

"Could we not exhibit him here?"

"Here? Why no. These premises, which all persons of refinement like myself find mean enough, would be a terror to the kind of menial dross I'm talking of. You see, there is an art in pleasing the masses—"

"An art, is it?" Claffey said.

"Yes, because by comparison with the masses, philosophers and dukes are easy prey. The problem with the populace is that people are always passing off on them, I mean you get some five-foot fly-by-night standing on a tree-stump, 'Oh, I'm a giant,' you get some goitered cretin passing himself off as the Freak That God Forgot—well, it won't do. Just because a man's lousy it doesn't mean he's a fuck-wit too, it doesn't mean he's a moon-calf just because he's poor. No, what the wider public requires is an honest product, bring them a freak and let it be a sound and genuine freak like Charlie here." Constantine nudged the Giant with his toe. "Is he asleep, or pretending? Then the other thing is, with the public, you must suit them, you must coddle them, you must slowly considerate about them; when you take their money you must make them feel they're in their own lice-shot parlours."

"Hence the cellar."

"Hence and hence. So get over to Slig."

"I still say it will be slow work, building up a sack. Maybe we ought to scour as well, see can we find Joe."

"You know he will have spent it," Con said patiently. "For you know Joe Vance. The man is a dilettante. He is a snapper-up. A man shows him a cravat at three times its worth, and oh, snap it up, says Joe, cravats like that are worth a king's ransom. How he ever got on in agenting is something I couldn't account for."

"You're right, bro," Claffey said. "Charlie's money will be gone on Canary wine, Chinese cabinets, and unstrung lutes. Moth collections behind glass, rambling roses, and tickets to the opera. That's what grieves me. I could have spent it on something sensible."

"Yes," Con nodded. "It could well be remarked of Joe Vance, that he had a sensibility above his income."

The Giant opened his eyes. He stared up at them, from the floor, his clear eyes turned backwards in his head. And spoke to this effect: "The Devil cannot genuflect, for backwards are his knees."

"Mester Howison, will you stand us a round?" Pybus shouted. "Our Giant is robbed and our agent gone, and our pockets are empty."

So, Pybus: neatly telling the man Howison everything he wished to know.

Ordering up the ale, Howison asked, "How's your Giant taking it?"

"He lies on the floor," said Con Claffey, "with his eyes and ears shut mostly."

"The poor man," said Howison thoughtfully.

"We will pay you back," said Claffey, "when we drive the Giant to work. My brother Con here, he has a scheme, about putting him in a cellar."

"And you have not heard the pretty part of it," said Con, settling with his pot in front of him. He smiled, and looked mysterious, as well as greasy.

Presently, Tibor the Terrible Tartar came in.

"The man himself," Con greeted him. "How's your prancer, Tibbsie?"

Tibor shook his head. He looked downcast. He was a little bow-legged man, grey in the face.

"Her ghost walks the amphitheatres," he said. "God bless her, Jenny. She was a horse and a half." An oily tear shone in his eye. "Nobody regards a Tartar with just one horse. Stand on the back at full gallop, swivel under belly, and shoot arrows, they think it's a mere nothing. I've had complaints and demanding their money back. I've had dung thrown."

"Lack of capital just now prevents our investment," Con Claffey said. "But it may not prevent it forever. Meanwhile, you were telling me about a human pincushion?"

"Yes." Tibor sat down, sighing, and rubbed his nose. "Whether it's a plague of agents absconding, or what it is, but there's a number of acts and shows floundering for want of investment—"

"And want of management," Con Claffey said. "Here, Mester Howison, won't you sit with us? You might be interested in this."

Howison, amiably commanding their pots filled, translated himself among them.

"So what have you got?"

"Pinheads," the Tartar replied. "Pinheads there for the harvesting. Three I know of alone, in a garret in Conduit Street, existing by the charity of their neighbours, too frail to venture out to get bread, and afraid of being stoned."

"Hm. These neighbours," said Con Claffey. "How much would they want?"

"Hardly a question at all," Tibor said. "They're not in the freak game, it seems they supply the pinheads just out of Christian charity."

Francis Claffey sniggered. "We'll send them a bouquet."

"And what else?"

Tibor wiped the back of his hand across his mouth. "There's a stone-eater wants managing."

"I've a scepticism," Con Claffey said, "about stone-eaters."

"No, it's right," said Tibor. "He eats up to a peck a day. If you dunt his belly you can hear them rattle. Paid a halfpenny, he will jump up and down for you and they rattle better."

Said Pybus—who had grown noticeably intelligent since Mary attacked him, as if all he needed was a blow to the head—"Do they not stop him up, the stones?"

"Ah," said Tibor. "Once in three weeks he takes some opening medicine, and voids a great quantity of sand."

"How does he do that?" said Howison.

"His stomach is equipped with a grinding mechanism."

Howison smiled.

"Just think." Beaming Con Claffey rubbed his hands. "All the cellars of London. A thousand cellars, and each fitted with a freak, and each freak bringing in a pound a day! Do you begin to see, Mester Howison? The potential?"

"I see it clearly," said Howison. "But what has it to do with me?"

"The life of a freak is not long," said Con. "Not once it has been brought to London and been worked. Now, Tibbsie, bear me out here."

"The life of a freak is not long," said Tibor the Terrible.

"You are thinking my master would be interested," Howison said. He took a long and pensive pull of his ale. "He might, at that."

"So we were thinking," said Francis Claffey.

"So we were thinking," his brother Con said, swooping fatly over his brother's words, "we were thinking that if Mr. Hunter would lay out on the initial capitalising of our cellars—for which we would cut a favourable deal with our countrymen—we could give him first refusal on the corpses."

"Mr. Hunter has no money to throw about, you understand? Besides, I don't know that . . . I'm not sure that he . . ." Howison lapsed into silent thought.

Respectful of it, all the companions took a long drink.

In the end, Howison said, "But I'd be interested. I myself."

For, he thinks, any corpse I come by, I can always sell on to John-o at a rate which will make me a small but interesting profit. He always has no money, but there are sources he can draw on, if I remind him early enough. Borrow from his admirers, why not? He has many. And he will always raise cash to buy the things he really wants to cut up.

John-o is interested in cutting up whatever he finds at the limits of life. He is interested in what distinguishes plants from animals, and animals from man. The latter distinction, Howison thinks, may need more than a scalpel to make it.

But he keeps such thoughts to himself. He turns back to the Irish, wreathed in smiles.

"By God, man," said Hunter, pulling down the Giant's eyelid.

"What is it? What do you see?"

"What do *you* see?" asked John.

The Giant had come out to the knock: to the peremptory rap of a man who expected the door answered. He'd thought it might be the law. I am large enough, he'd thought, to knock down the law of England. Thought it without self-promotion. Only sad fact.

Hunter had been stamping there, scrappy and mere and bluff. "I come to see how you do, Charles Byrne."

"Go before me," said the Giant, courteous. "There will be no charge. My minders aren't here, and by now, I should say, I regard you almost as a personal friend."

Hunter stepped in, and looked around. "I am afraid they have sold the tea-caddy," said the Giant, "and all its contents. Or I could offer you . . ."

"No matter," said the Scot.

He took a seat. "That one has a dint in the back," the Giant said.

"No matter."

"I once wept, sitting in that chair."

"For what reason?"

"I don't recall."

"Your memory fails?"

"Everything fails, sir. Reason, and harvests, and the human heart."

For a moment Hunter stared at him, oddly. "I wonder," he said. "That is a fine set of satirical prints you have got on your wall there. Might they be for sale?"

"Possibly," said the Giant. "Quite probably, in fact. What the late Joe Vance thought of as a satire, is not precisely my idea of the term."

Hunter shifted uneasily in the dinted chair. "And what would your idea be?"

"Properly understood, a satire can blister the face of the man it's made against. It can fish out his soul and spit it on the tip of a knife."

"Well, if one could," the Scotchman said, regretting. "If such a manoeuvre were possible."

"It may be," the Giant said, "that you don't have the right kind of knife."

Hunter conceded. He sat nodding his head, balding, with the frippery bits of cheek-ginger bristling, like scragged lace, against the failing light of a fine spring evening.

"Drink, sir?" said the Giant. "From our decanter? Or is it too early for you?"

"Oh, why not, why not?" said Hunter. No danger, tonight, that he would go whoopsy-hic. He was concentrated now; you could pour in a distillery and it wouldn't dizzy him.

The Giant bestowed a glass of decent crystal, and within it

what tasted like a decent claret—but what would he know? Probably Wullie would have damned it. But Wullie was dead.

"Are you quite well, Mr. Hunter?"

He was aware that the Giant was gazing down at him.

"My brother Wullie has passed away."

"That's a sad circumstance, Mr. Hunter. I'm sorry to hear it."

The little man took a sip from his glass. Then he put it down. "Let's not get sentimental." He looked up. His eyes were slicing; the Giant thought, he has some kind of blade, at least. "I'll put it to you straight," he said. "You're a dead man. Is that clear?"

"I feel yet," said the Giant, "the bronzed, the bloody ocean swim within me, its waters crazed with wrecks; the slapping seas, that are mad with the merman's murmur." He thought, that's a foul line, merman's murmur: heroic foul. "My eyes see—sometimes. My tongue—from time to time—continues to speak."

"Yes, man, but you are doomed. Your heart is laboring, your liver swollen, your limbs—as you know—extending."

"Dear Sir Hunter," said the Giant. "For a long time now, I have deceived my followers . . . and may God forgive me. I held out the hope that my growth might make me a more valuable exhibit. Patrick O'Brien—"

"Yes, I've heard of him," the Scot rapped out. "He is embarked and embarked, but where is he?"

"It's a mystery," said the Giant. "Like Toby, the Sapient Pig. Both, believe me, will appear amongst us; but not yet."

"Like signs," Hunter said. "Do you feel it so?"

"I feel every bloody thing," said the Giant. "I am notorious for what I feel. Come on, Mr. Hunter, I am inviting you in civil, I am giving you such refreshment as lies within my situation, and you are not such a fool but that you do not know that in this last month my fortune has taken a turn for the worse." Charlie rubbed his head. "As yours, of course, with the death of your brother."

"I'll talk no more of Wullie." Hunter swayed his head, side to side like a dog. "I've a proposition."

The Giant closed his eyes. "Make it," he said. He drew back his lips, in a kind of friendliness; he breathed deep, and a pulse jumped, deep within the flesh of his cheek, and controlled his smile.

Hunter began to speak. Within a second—for desire must be held back—he choked on his wine. O'Brien would have leaned forward and slapped him on the back; but Hunter was a frail strange creature, and the Giant feared to dismember him like a butterfly, dust him apart like a dried moth.

Then the man Hunter made his proposition.

The Giant listened, and placed his wine-glass with great care on the side-table. A jewelled inch was left, in which lees hung like crushed roaches in amber.

"Excuse me," he said. He then lay down on his back. He closed his eyes and he closed his ears.

"Ah well," said the man Hunter.

Was I not kind to him? thought the Giant.

Did I not usher him, warning him against the dint chair?

Did I not give what hospitality was in me?

Hunter was uncertain what to do. Stared down. Measured the Giant, coveted him, and yet felt himself in a situation of some social unease. Try again another day?

The Giant said only, "Get out. Cromwellian."

Hunter walks back to Jermyn Street, his brain working. In the hall, he turns out his pockets. One shilling and sixpence. Hm. He calls out, "Anne, are you up there? Got any money?"

Fifty pounds ought to do it, he thinks. He cogitates the sum, revolves it. He would, of course, have offered less, but they had not got to the stage of mentioning figures before Byrne had lain down and ceased to participate. As if it were unreasonable!

He hears his own voice—"Why beat about the bush? You're

dying and you're on your uppers. You want money, I want your bones. It's a simple enough transaction to comprehend. I send my man around with an agreed sum in cash. And in return, you put your thumb-print to a compact we'll draw up, saying I'm to have your corpse. So you see the advantage I'm offering you?" He paused. "Have the money while you're alive and can enjoy it. Man, ye may as well."

He thought he'd explained it clearly enough. But before he'd finished talking, something had fallen out of the man's features. Some kind of understanding. Leaving a great blank. Wiped.

"Look at it this way," he'd said encouragingly. "It's your chance to contribute to the sum of human knowledge, after you're gone. If you don't want the money yourself you could distribute it among your followers. Or send it back to your relatives."

The man said—and in his voice there was no expression at all—"I could apply it to charitable purposes. The relief of indigent freaks."

"Ye could, at that," said John.

Then the man asked him, oddly, "This contract, will it be written in English?"

"Of course," he said.

The Giant said, "I thought it might." Then he lay down on the floor.

Hunter hugs himself. He knows he can get this giant, somehow. If the price is right. He'll have to borrow, of course.

No answer from his wife. Mr. Bach—or one of his offspring—is tripping down the stairs.

What's the Giant doing, when he lies on the floor? There is a point—and you may know it yourself—a point in fatigue or pain when logic slowly crumbles from the world, where reason's bricks sieve to crumb. Where content flits from language, goes its ways and departs, its pack on its back: you take the high road and I'll take the low. Where meaning evaporates into the air like ether.

The Giant has reached this point. When he seals his senses, he's sealing out the meaningless, because inside he's trying to preserve some sense of what meaning means. He examines the words. He interrogates them. Bones. Compact. Corpse. But finally, here's why he's lying on the floor. No fancy reasons. Forget philosophy. He's lying on the floor because he's realised this, that there's nothing to be done. There's simply *nothing.*

There's
simply
nothing
to be done.

But the Giant rises: and to vituperate. To say, curse him, John Hunter, he thinks I can't read. To smash the satires out of their frames, to splinter the rattling sash, to hurl against the stained wall the three-legged stool that of its very nature don't wobble: for God help us, in this quaking sin-sodden world, why should tripods be privileged?

The Giant's voice is shaking the beams. He is smashing the glass from here to Fleet Street. He is setting up quivers in the foundations that will crack down Cockspur Street, one fine day; vibrations that will blow London apart.

"Will I take him on in a contest?" he howls. "Trigonometry? Or singing? Will the dog match me, God rot him, in Socratic dialogue? I tell you what it is." He turns, his face blazing, his feet pounding the boards; we can expect soon a billet-doux from the tenants below. "It's a new and original wickedness. To come to a man, to say 'I'll buy you,' to say 'I'll buy you while you're still breathing, I'll buy you now against the hour of your death.' "

"Not so," said narrow Slig.

"How not so?"

"Not so because it ain't," drawled Con Claffey. "Not new, not original. Not wicked, even."

"Enlarge," the Giant demanded.

"It is a familiar pretext," said Con, "for anatomies to approach those felons about to be hanged—among which company we may enumerate ourselves one day—"

He paused, and waited for a comradely titter: which proceeded, in the end, from Tibor the Terrible Tartar. "They approach those felons, I say—and offer to purchase their corpses in advance, so that they may have a good suit to hang in."

"Jesus," said Slig. "You remember Sixteen-String Joe?"

"Jesus, do I," said Con. "What a figure he cut, when he was bound in the cart. Joe was a redoubtable highwayman, a land-pirate of the first water. He departed this life with his hair curled, and his waistcoat embroidered with the flowers of the forest, the pearls of the sea. By God, and with an ode in his mouth. He croacked well, did Joe."

"So it's regular?" said the Giant. He wanted to think the approach of the little Scotsman was some stealthy, snuffling seduction, peculiar to him. Their faces showed him the truth: it's regular.

He thought, where's Joe Vance?

Where's he lying tonight?

I wish he were by me now.

Good old Joe.

Money or not.

Would agent, but never sell me.

Sack of lucre.

Never do it now. Mulroney's. Never the lyre-backed chairs. And horribly enough, that's what Joe understood. He knew what was beautiful. He knew what would last. And he thefted his own vision. Go explain that.

twelve

Jankin stood stock-still, regarding the Spotted Boy. Studying him. The boy looked about twelve years old. He was kept undressed to show his pigmentation; grey-white patches against dull brown. Old scars laced his body, thin black ropy scars; from cuts, from worms, from insect bites that had festered. But it was his patches that distinguished him, and Jankin remembered the black man he had seen on the quay on his first morning in England.

"See." His grin shot over his shoulder. He almost said, Joe Vance, Joe Vance. "See, I told you. Told you it would rub off. Rub off more," he advised the Spotted Boy. "Then you'll be white and a free man like me."

. . .

Down in that cellar where the freaks cluster, that's where they're to be found, the Giant and Jankin and Pybus who is only a boy. They were drawn there by Claffey's ambition to become an agent, and from now on it's among these freaks they will live, crawling back at night to Cockspur Street to their lousy beds. Nobody was doing the housekeeping these days. Bitch Mary was hatching a bastard, her frame broadening and coarsening to accommodate it. "Let me have twenty children," she said, sneering. "Then I can sell my boys to chimney-sweeps and my girls to Drury Lane snatch-purveyors."

It was not surprising to find that the landlord Kane was in the freak racket. It turned out he owned the garret where the pinheads clustered, and—by extension—owned the pinheads. He had not been working them because of a glut on the market, "but won't I dust off the little devils?" he said. "By God, Con, it's a prime plan. Let all the monster-makers of this city co-ordinate their efforts, let the trick-trainers move in concert. Meet Fernando, will you?"

Fernando was a young man of twenty-six or so, with flippers where others have arms and legs. He spoke in a high bright voice, his lips pulled savagely back in a smile that was very like a snarl. "Fernando," he said, "will play at ninepins. Fernando will shoot a bow and arrow. Fernando will play the flute. Thread a needle." A drop of foaming spittle whipped itself across the room. "Fernando will dress his own hair."

"We have some savages," Kane explained. "They're not real ones. We have to pin their tails on before we can start the show. We did have some real ones, but they died in the cold weather."

Claffey said, interested, "What does a savage do?"

"Basically," Kane said, "they eat toads and flies, bite the heads off rats and chickens, and suck their blood. If you can't find real savages from overseas you have to find Londoners that know no better. If you can find them mad enough, they will go down on four legs and bark like a dog."

And coming and going in that cellar and others, in White Hart Lane and Bedfordbury, in Smock Alley and Bow Street, they met the fire-eaters and the posture-masters who perform contortions; with the amiable grey-faced Tibor as conductor and guide, they met Sham Sam the Conjuror, and men dressed as monkeys, and monkeys dressed as bearded ladies. "All these people are my friends," Tibor said. "As for the savages, some of them come from extinct lines. They sing songs, lamenting how they are the last of their tribes."

"Tribes of Whitechapel," snorted Con Claffey. "Tribes of Seven Dials. How's your nephew, Sam, got over the measles yet?"

"Mending, thank you," said Sham Sam. "My nephew's the Son of a Cannibal, you know. Well, we used to show him as the Cannibal himself, gnawing a rabbit bone and saying it was a young child. But then a woman who was in pod took a screaming fit, and threatened us with fetching the Lord Mayor. So we've dropped him down a generation. Now we give him a bone and he toys with it. Looks at it wistful. You know. Like he would suck it, if he dared."

That day, they had been teaching the pinheads to bow. A flourish of the wrist, arm drawn neatly across chest, palm spread, then a low sway from the hips. It made a change for the pinheads. Usually they just sat in a corner, looking listless.

They are wonders, they are prodigies, the Giant tells them; they are nature's curlicues and flourishes, extravagances of flesh. He moved among them, carefully, the fruit of God's absent-mindedness: the web-footed ones, the ones with sloped heads and fish mouths, the ones with great wobbling heads and loose yellow skin dropping from their frames in folds: the ones with strange growths, the bird-faces, and the bat's faces with folded eyes.

Jankin said, whispering to him, "Charlie O'Brien, I never thought it—but there's lower than Irish."

The Giant looked at him, his tow-head and vacant face—a hair's breadth from exhibition himself.

"Jankin, you wouldn't sell me, would you?" he asked. In a low voice. For he had begun to suspect it.

Jankin's face was perplexed, but then his expression cleared. "Oh well," he said. "I'm threatened to tell you nothing at all about anything of that." He tapped the side of his nose.

"I see," the Giant said.

At night he dreamt of the freaks, their pug-noses and protruding tongues, the characters set free from his stories; and Francis Claffey in his crib dreamt of the pennies mounting up.

The Giant has learned this lesson: anything you can imagine, can exist.

The Giant was sicker. He had grown by three or four inches (and still Paddy did not come). There was constant pain in his fingers and feet, his skin was stretched, and his head ached. His skin had a low shine on it, like pewter. At nights he coughed, with a sound that roared down Cockspur Street like cannon fire.

"You were a stubborn fool," Claffey said to him, "not to take the Scot's money."

The Giant watched him. What double game is this?

"I might re-consider," he said. "I doubt I have three months in me. I'd like to have once more a sack on my back. I could give the runt the slip, and go back and die in Ireland."

He watched a pale rage washing to and fro through Claffey's eyes, slap slap slap like the water in some dirty tributary of the Thames.

"Ye'll never," Claffey said. "You're done for, you're shot. Face up to it, O'Brien. You couldn't take the voyage."

Now he understood Claffey's game; it was to place his intentions precisely; it was to understand them. It was to see if he knew he was dying. "And besides," Claffey said, "the word is out that Hunter's withdrawn the offer."

"Oh yes?"

"Yes. He's more interested in pinheads these days."

"Then he shouldn't have long to wait. The way you starve the poor little brutes."

"Ah, they get their wibble and slop. It's what they understand. You couldn't give them meat. Their teeth are out."

Claffey went downstairs, whistling. It's fact, the Giant told himself. Cold and stark. They mean to sell you.

John Hunter was in his counting house, counting out his money.

Thirty-four pounds, seven shillings, and a halfpenny.

Howison came in. "They say they are willing to guard him, till he's dead."

"And guard him *when* he's dead."

"Yes, that too." Howison cleared his throat. "They want a hundred guineas."

John hurtled forward, into space. He knocked his head hard on the corner of his dissecting bench.

He knelt on the boards, bleeding and swearing.

Meanwhile the Giant watched the Human Pincushion at work, seated on the three-legged stool, casually popping the pins in her mouth and swallowing. "Done it all me life," she explained, between bites. "Can't flourish at all without I have a nice pin in me mouth—or a needle's a treat. I like a nice darning needle when I can get one."

"Do they ever come out?" Pybus said, gaping.

"Oh yes. No show without they come out. First you see a black spot, like, on me arm or me leg, and then it festers a bit, then after a while you can see the head of the pin and so draw it out. A doctor comes and sees me, he asks to examine me, he says, Mrs.

Cricklewell, you're going to lose the use of your legs, and I says to him, Doctor, you just keep the pins coming and never mind legs, a woman has to earn a crust, and I says to him, What about my insomnia? Cure that, can you? Thing is, I have to be up in the night, scraping about for another mouthful."

"I have an iron-eater," Kane said, boasting. "Spectators are requested to bring items they want eaten, like a horseshoe, or a bunch of keys they don't need anymore."

"Ferris has a green man," Slig said. "He's showing him at Russell Street."

"How the hell would Ferris know if he's green? Ferris is blind."

"Ferris has vowed bloody revenge on the killers of Bride Caskey."

Claffey spat. "Let him come round here, and bring his verdant freak. He'll be green himself when I've kicked him in the groin."

"In the reign of Conaire," said the Giant, "there was no dissension in the land. Every man thought his neighbour's voice as sweet as a harp-string. In those summers, the sun shone unclouded from spring till October. Acorns were so abundant that men waded in them up to their knees. No wolf stole more than one bull-calf from any herd."

"So what went wrong?" Con Claffey said, yawning hugely.

"It was a matter of Conaire's foster brothers, apparently. Who were very fond of thieving and plundering."

"They could not be denied," said Pybus: not without admiration in his tone.

"At Da Dergha's Hostel," the Giant said, "when he and his followers were sitting down to feast, a woman came to them, a giant woman wearing a fleecy striped mantle. She had a beard that reached down to her knees, and her mouth was on one side of her head. She stood leaning on the doorpost, casting her eyes on the king and all the youths around him. 'What do you see?' the king asked her. She said"—and here the Giant paused, and seemed to choke on his words. "She said her name was Cailb.

“ ‘That is a short name,’ said the king.

“She said, ‘I have others. They are Samuin. Sinand. Seschend. Saiglend. Samlocht.’ ”

“Less names,” said Claffey. “And get on with it.”

The Giant glared. “Very well, Francis Claffey—if you don’t know what to call your fate when she comes for you, don’t come crying to me. There are at least twenty-six names I have not told you, so consider them all listed, and bear in mind that all these names she recited in one breath, and while standing on one leg.”

“Why did she do that?” Pybus asked.

“Why does anybody do anything? So Conaire asked her, ‘What do you want,’ and she said, ‘To come in.’ Conaire said, ‘There is a solemn prohibition placed on me against admitting any single woman after sunset.’ ”

“You mean no one had wed her?” Kane said. “And with a beard like that?”

“Solemn prohibition?” Con Claffey said. “The lad was making an excuse.”

“He was not,” said Jankin. “There was a solemn probibition, and you would know about it if you had ever listened to this tale with attention. He can’t catch birds either, bad luck to him if he does.”

“So the woman said to him, ‘I claim hospitality from this house.’ ”

The Giant thought, I let Hunter in. I wined the man.

“So Conaire said, ‘If I send you an ox or a salted pig, would you not go elsewhere?’

“Then the woman got angry, and she said, ‘A pretty pass for this nation, if the High King can’t offer a bed and a dinner to one lone woman.’ ”

“I quite agree,” said Mrs. Cricklewell.

“So Conaire said, ‘Let her in.’ And all the company was stricken with a great terror, though none of them knew why.”

"I know why," said Jankin. "Wouldn't anybody be terrified if there came in this great woman with a beard and her mouth on one side?"

Pybus said, "I wouldn't be frightened of a woman. Though I'd be frightened of that man who came in the ship, yesterday. The man with one great eye, and seven pupils in it, and all as black as beetles."

"Yes," said the Giant, "you were not here for that part of the tale, Con Claffey."

Con Claffey curled his lip.

"And I worry about those men with three heads," Pybus said. "And each head, three rows of teeth from ear to ear. And bones without joints."

"Are they for purchase?" said Slig.

Kane gnawed his lip. "There were fearful prodigies, in those days."

"Right, Kane. And in these days too." The Giant stood up. "I will not finish this tale."

"Temper, temper," said Mrs. Cricklewell.

"Right," the Giant bellowed, from the doorway. "Will I tell you what the woman said, as she stood on one leg? Will I tell you what she said? She said, 'I see your destruction, your utter destruction: you will not leave this house, none of you, neither hide nor hair, except for the fragments that are carried out in the claws of birds.' "

He turned away. His bitter shoulder. He heard Con Claffey say, in a low tone, "The fella's on to us. He comprehends our scheme."

He heard Slig say, "No matter. What can he do?"

And Kane: "They say the crocus is panting like a bride. Howison will drive the price up. We've got him on a percentage. It's in his interest."

At Jermyn Street, Howison attended his master's gashed scalp, all the time talking to him soothingly. "Try the eminences. Apply to the worthies. Money will forthcome. You must have that giant."

And by the fireside, Slig: "I have known men and women who were exceptionally hairy."

Says Kane, "I have known a salamander, lives up Tooley Street. He has a sister would eat live coals as some eat sugar plums."

The Giant thinks, I have known people with claws instead of hands. They terrorise people. Their mother loves them but they murder her, so what then? They go out in the world murdering.

Mrs. Cricklewell bites on a bodkin. Crack, crack, crack. A splinter falls from her lip.

Protect me, thinks the Giant. Breastplate and shield. King Conaire and all his men.

Slig says, "At Petticoat Lane we have a thing called What Is It."

"And what is it?" Claffey asks.

"That is what you cannot know, nor I divulge. It is a thing beyond decribing. We keep it behind a curtain, and charge extra."

"Can we see it?" Claffey looks eager.

"That you cannot."

In the stories, a giant has a cap which makes him disappear. He has slippers that take him around the world in minutes.

What had Bride Caskey said? In England they hunt them down with large dogs.

Negotiations are in progress. The Giant's price is driving up and up. Heads are whispering together at the Crown on Wych Street. Two hundred, three. John-o near-apoplectic. Howison's part in this should not be inspected too closely. Slig is planning on extending his cellar empire to the east. Tibor the Terrible hopes to get a new horse out of it. "I'll call her Jenny," he says, sentimentally. "Set men closely about him," Hunter begs.

Says Howison, "They are close."

Hunter makes an itching motion with his fingers. "I should like to examine him. To see how near the end. But he would not admit me." He sucks his lip. "Not even for half a crown."

The Giant: "If only I could get a good poet. Somebody to recite at him. A good poet can recite a man to death. A poet takes a person's earlobe between his finger and thumb and grinds it, and straight away that person dies. With a wisp of hay and a cross word they drive a man demented. They chew flesh and set it on the threshold and when a man steps over it he drops to his knees and expires."

The Spotted Boy comes in, bearing a message. It's late May and he's shivering. There's a smoky ring around the pupils of his eyes. Slig looks knowing. "Another for the knacker's," he says, when the Spotted Boy goes out.

"God curse him!" cries the Giant. "If he cuts me up, I cannot rise again."

"But your throne in heaven!" Jankin says. "The cushions of scarlet silk! Stuffed with the down of a thousand swans! Tassels is in it. And jewels the size of soup-plates."

"Yes," says the Giant shortly. "It is prepared for me, Jankin, for I never hurt any creature. But if my bones are dispersed, I cannot have it."

Jankin's mind is moving slowly, theologically. "And cannot you go to hell either?"

The Giant shakes his head. "I can go nowhere. Nothing is to go. Dead is dead, for me."

Jankin says, shaken, "I had not thought of this. Does Mr. Hunter know?"

The Giant stared hard at him. "Hunter has no god. What is faith? He cannot anatomise it. What is hope? He cannot boil its bones. What is charity—aye, what is charity, to a bold experimentalist such as he?"

Jankin's face was white. "I did not realise it, Charlie. That you could not rise."

"Jankin, would you bury me at sea? Would you place me in a casket of lead?"

Jankin began to weep.

"I did not realise it," he said. "God forgive me, Charles O'Brien. It is a thing I did not know."

The Giant rocks himself a little.

He thinks: no person rocked me, I was a giant child. The cradle would have burst.

Here I am: a man grown.

What could his life have been, if he had not been a giant? He might have been a poor scholar, wandering the roads; his cloth satchel on his back, the shape of his books evident through them, so every traveller he met, and every householder whose door he visited would recognise his calling, and any stranger would offer him a place at the hearth. He might have made his life on the roads, a useful man and a hired dreamer, offering his services in each settlement for the writing of letters and the drawing of leases; stopping in some place he liked the look of, to hold school in the hedge and conference under the tree, to dance at the tavern and sharpen his wits on the priest, to court the girls and beat into the boys the principles of geometry and the alphabet in Greek. He might have been a poet and diviner; lying in the dark, his hands crossed over his face to shut out any beam of light: until the light dawns inwards, and the poem is cracked open. He might have bathed in the five streams of the fountain of wisdom, and kept company with the night-visiting gods.

But instead it is fetch the water from the pump, the flat slimy water; it is the hit of cheap gin in the gullet, and Claffey's fumbling feet on the stair. It is the Scotchman waiting, idly jingling the coins in his pocket; it is the animal-trainer, flicking his whip. The harpers play three strains: smile, wail, and sleep. But these nights as he lies awake, the deep ache springing from his bones, he hears the rattle of the nightwatchman, like the chattering of God's teeth. He hears the wheels of the coach of death, rumbling over the cobbles, and he knows that if he were to stir and open the shutter, he would see the headless horses, and death's coachman with his basin of blood.

The poet has his memorial in repetition, and the statesman in stone and bronze. The scholar's hand lies always on his book, and the thinker's eyes on canvas travel the room to rest on each human face; the rebel has his ballad and his cross, his bigot's garland, his wreath of rope. But for the poor man and the giant there is the scrubbed wooden slab and the slop bucket, there is the cauldron and the boiling pot, and the dunghill for his lights; so he is a stench in the nose for a day or a week, so he is a no-name, so he is oblivion. Stories cannot save him. When human memory runs out, there is the memory of animals; behind that, the memory of the plants, and behind that the memory of the rocks. But the wind and the sea wear the rocks away; and the cell-line runs to its limit, where meaning falls away from it, and it loses knowledge of its own nature. Unless we plead on our knees with history, we are done for, we are lost. We must step sideways, into that country where space plaits and knots, where time folds and twists: where the years pass in a day.

June comes. The stinking streets. O'Brien tosses through the night, wringing the sheet, twisting it and soiling it with his death-sweat. He prays for mayhem to break out, for the rebels to take the field; he prays for the Whiteboys to come, swooping in, smashing with billhook and pike: Slasher, Cropper, Night Errant: Thumper, Madcap Setfire, and Captain Right. To the rescue.

Slig says, to the Spotted Boy, "Tell Kane. Not long now."

Jankin is crying in the corner.

The Spotted Boy says to him, "If I were white like you and a free man, how would I earn my living?"

Says Slig, "Tell Hunter he refuses food. Tell him he persistently curses and swears. Tell him our guard is strong and our hearts are true. Tell him the price is five hundred pounds."

Hunter says, "Do they want my blood?"

The Giant, raving on the floor, wishes him skulls and entrails strewn, wishes him cold winds and scalping blades: the fall of a house, the loss of heirs, an abundance of spectres, a rejoicing of crows. A high gallows and a windy day.

He says, "Did you ever hear of the army of men with cats' heads?"

Jankin says, "Would you give us Ebinichebel, King of the Dog-Heads?"

The Giant says, "I am too weak for that vile Saracen."

An hour passes. Slig and Con Claffey, they are bristling and alert. Says Kane, "Soon we shall swagger."

As the evening cools, he rallies a little. He says, "There was once a race of people called the Astomi. They had no mouths. They lived on the smell of apples."

Standing in the shadows, waiting for him, are Katherine Lineham and Ruggetty Madge, Teddy Brian and Redman Keogh: Cooley and Ryan and Thomas Dwyer, that came from Tipperary and had no coat to his back.

But he dies to the sound of What Is It, dragging its chain in the next room.

. . .

One day, about a week later—when the Giant's bones, boiled brown, were already hanging in the workshop of the impoverished John Hunter—Pybus and Jankin were crossing Drury Lane, on their way to become drunk at the Fox Tavern. Ducking round a cart, Jankin was nearly bowled over by a spry black pig that shot from an alley. The pig checked its pace, darted a glance over its shoulder, and with its trotter performed a quick calculation on the cobbles.

A vast excitement swelled inside Pybus. "Toby!" he yelled. "It's Mester Goss's pig!" He made a lunge for it. The pig side-stepped him; but then it halted, and once more glanced back. It seemed to be smirking.

Jankin skidded to a halt on the cobbles. "Toby," he yelled. "Toby, here, lad." From under his coat he fished the halter that Joe had bade him prepare, for the day when the pig should arrive. Still Toby lurked, and shifted his feet, as if he knew something.

"By God," said Jankin. "It has a look in its eye."

Puzzled, Pybus replied, "Yes. So it does."

The two men stood watching each other. "We could easy catch it," Jankin said. "For look at it; it's standing there, waiting for what will we do."

"Yes," Pybus said. "We could easy catch it."

Thoughtfully, he rubbed his grazed knees.

"On for the Fox, is it?" Jankin said.

Pybus nodded. "On for the Fox."

Toby, performing another rapid addition, wheeled smartly and trotted off towards Long Acre. Jankin and Pybus raised their hands in salute.

King Conaire had a singing sword. Do you know this? He was the son of a bird-god.

His head spoke after it was severed. Thank you, it said. Thank you for listening.

Put away the dark lantern and the hooks. Coil the rope ladder, and roll up the sacks. Clean your shovel before you stow it; you'll be wanting it again.

The Lancet, 1937: "Sir Joshua Reynolds's portrait of John Hunter . . . is gradually disappearing. . . . Fading has advanced unchecked. The change is greatest below. The surroundings of the figure are so dim as to be indecipherable; the legs are almost indistinguishable, the pendent right hand resembles a shapeless pudding, the pen that it held is gone. The face, the least affected part, has lost its once sharp outline—a change that enhances its absorbed, far-away expression. . . . The whole picture is progessing towards extinction."

I want a crow's nest, and a magpie's nest, and the branches of the tree they are set in. I cannot get a large porpoise for love or money. I want some eels and they must not come from a fishmonger, but straight from the river.

I had three hedgehogs, and all have died.

I want some ostrich eggs. And a bittern, to hear it boom, and learn how it makes that noise.

. . .

I want knowledge. I want time.

And time wants you, John. You will become a grain of wheat. You will be changed to a pool of water. To a worm, a fly. And a wind will blow the fly away.